"Who are you, Amelia? Why are you here?"

"Your parents—"

"They could have hired a nurse or a sitter for me. Why you?"

She shook her head gently.

"You're carrying my baby, aren't you?"

Her gaze met his and fell. She moved toward the window. He followed her, determined to know.

When she stopped and turned, he was right there by her side. She looked up into his eyes and said, "Yes."

"Then why aren't we married?"

She was silent again. He could see her trying to come up with answers he would like, and it irritated him. "Just tell me the truth, Amelia!"

"The truth? Is that what you really want?"

"Yes," he answered without hesitation, but suddenly he was filled with doubt....

Dear Reader,

The year 2000 marks the twentieth anniversary of Silhouette Books! Ever since May 1980, Silhouette Books—and its flagship line, Silhouette Romance—has published the best in contemporary category romance fiction. And the year's stellar lineups across *all* Silhouette series continue that tradition.

This month in Silhouette Romance, Susan Meier unveils her miniseries BREWSTER BABY BOOM, in which three brothers confront instant fatherhood after inheriting six-month-old triplets! First up is *The Baby Bequest,* in which Evan Brewster does diaper duty…and learns a thing or two about love from his much-younger, mommy-in-the-making assistant. In Teresa Southwick's charming new Silhouette Romance novel, a tall, dark and handsome man decides to woo a jaded nurse *With a Little T.L.C. The Sheik's Solution* is a green-card marriage to his efficient secretary in this lavish fairy tale from Barbara McMahon.

Elizabeth Harbison's CINDERELLA BRIDES series continues with the magnificent *Annie and the Prince.* In Cara Colter's dramatic *A Babe in the Woods,* a mystery man arrives on a reclusive woman's doorstep with a babe on his back—and a gun in his backpack! Then we have a man without a memory who returns to his *Prim, Proper… Pregnant* former fiancée—this unique story by Alice Sharpe is a must-read for those who love twists and turns.

In coming months, look for special titles by longtime favorites Diana Palmer, Joan Hohl, Kasey Michaels, Dixie Browning, Phyllis Halldorson and Tracy Sinclair, as well as many newer but equally loved authors. It's an exciting year for Silhouette Books, and we invite you to join the celebration!

Happy reading!

Mary-Theresa Hussey

Mary-Theresa Hussey
Senior Editor

Please address questions and book requests to:
Silhouette Reader Service
U.S.: 3010 Walden Ave., P.O. Box 1325, Buffalo, NY 14269
Canadian: P.O. Box 609, Fort Erie, Ont. L2A 5X3

PRIM, PROPER...
PREGNANT

Alice Sharpe

Silhouette

R O M A N C E™

Published by Silhouette Books

America's Publisher of Contemporary Romance

This book is dedicated with love to Joyce Sharpe.

 SILHOUETTE BOOKS

ISBN 0-373-19425-0

PRIM, PROPER... PREGNANT

Visit us at www.romance.net

Printed in U.S.A.

Books by Alice Sharpe

Silhouette Romance

Going to the Chapel #1137
Missing: One Bride #1212
Wife on His Doorstep #1304
Prim, Proper... Pregnant #1425

Silhouette Yours Truly

If Wishes Were Heroes

ALICE SHARPE

met her husband-to-be on a cold, foggy beach in Northern California. One year later they were married. Their union has survived the rearing of two children, a handful of earthquakes registering over 6.5, numerous cats and a few special dogs, the latest of which is a yellow Lab named Annie Rose. Alice and her husband now live in a small rural town in Oregon, where she devotes the majority of her time to pursuing her second love, writing.

Alice loves to hear from readers. You can write her at P.O. Box 755 Brownsville, OR 97327. SASE for reply is appreciated.

Chapter One

After ten minutes of furtive searching, Amelia Enderling was about to give up. She paused near an open door, hoping for a fortifying glance at the bay, and that was when she finally spotted him. He was standing near the rock wall that skirted the terrace of the Bayview Country Club, looking toward the sea.

She couldn't have asked for a better opportunity. After all, he was alone. Now was the moment to rush forward, blurt out the truth, then disappear from Seaport, Oregon, forever. So why did she stand as still as one of the cement planters overflowing with lilac petunias and white alyssum, just staring?

It had been four months since she'd last seen him. Four months, two weeks, three days. He was still outrageously good-looking—slender, yet with broad shoulders and obvious strength beneath the fine fabric of the tuxedo he wore as best man at his older brother's wedding. His hair was as dark as a moonless night, slightly wavy, brushed away from a high forehead. His lashes were long, his

brown eyes deep pools, his nose and chin perfectly
formed and absolutely masculine. Standing as he was,
thoughtful and reposed, he looked aristocratic and yet
sensual, like a seductive monarch in a fairy-tale land
awaiting the arrival of a beautiful consort.

He was a lawyer.

Amelia glanced down at her cornflower blue dress,
wishing suddenly she'd thought to wear a concealing
sweater no matter how warm the July day promised to
be. Too late. She was stalling.

It wasn't until she felt his eyes on her that she looked
up and met his gaze. Her breath caught in her throat.
She'd always known she was physically attracted to
him—it was one of the major reasons she'd put off this
encounter for so long—but she'd assumed that after what
he'd done to her, knowing what she knew of him, the
effect would be minimal. Ha!

It was as though a million invisible wires pulsed between them, sending signals from his body to hers, reliv-
ing the past, speculating on the future. In that glance was
the feel of his skin, the taste of his lips, the heat of his
mouth, the desire. It was all she could do to make herself
take a step in his direction when every fiber in her being
urged her to turn around and run.

She told herself that Ryder was like a vase of cut flowers, all show, rootless, and over an extended period of
time, sure to wilt. She told herself he was a mannequin,
not a man, that he was selfish and if she allowed it, he
would hurt her again and not even know it.

He smiled at her as though this was their first meeting,
as though the past didn't exist. No matter what Ryder the
man was like, no matter how deceiving he could be, his
smile seemed to spring like well water from the depths

of the earth, pure and simple and damn near impossible to resist.

She inhaled deeply, filling her lungs, and resisted.

He now looked puzzled. Well, in a few moments, she'd replace his expression with shock. Her step faltered as she approached him, but her resolve remained. It was now or never.

"Hello," he said in his deep voice that still made her tingle, a knee-jerk reaction she thoroughly resented. His greeting was like a caress, intimate, somehow hinting that fate had designed this moment. Not for the first time, Amelia found herself thinking that Ryder had missed his calling—he should have been an actor.

"I need to talk to you," she said.

Despite her abrupt response, a smile lingered on his beautiful lips. Leaning against the rock wall, arms crossed over his chest, his eyes full of life, he said, "Of course."

She stared at the white rosebud pinned to his lapel. Her mouth felt dry. "This is difficult," she said.

He furrowed his brow, as though confused as to why she would find talking to him awkward.

"Remember last March?" she mumbled.

His elegant eyebrows inched up his forehead. Amelia, whose face was already hot from the memory of the passionate night the two of them had spent stormbound in his apartment, felt even more flushed as he said, "Last March? Hmm…let me think."

The twinkle in his eye told her all she needed to know. He was teasing her, winking internally, letting her know *his* life was full of romantic interludes that involved fervent lovemaking and promises never meant to be taken seriously. There were just so many women last March, he seemed to say with that smile. Give me a second to sort through them all.

But she didn't give him a second. She placed her hand on his arm, a mistake she tried at once to rectify but which he halted by firmly placing his hand over hers and gently squeezing. As in the past, in fact, even more profoundly now, the touch of his warm fingers resounded through her body like a shout in a closet, and she involuntarily trembled.

She said, "Please. Please, just let me say this."

He nodded. "Go for it."

The fancy rehearsed words were gone, lost in a maelstrom of anxiety. She heard herself stammer, "I'm... well, I'm pregnant."

The relief! The words were finally out in the open air where they were free to sink or soar. She chanced a look at his face, expecting to see the beginnings of anger as her statement and all its implications struck home, but instead he looked wistful.

Wistful?

His gaze sweeping her fuller-than-ever bust and the bulge that was there in her midsection if you knew to look for it, he said, "Congratulations."

"What!"

He shook his head ever so slightly. "Congratulations. Isn't that what one says? You look radiant. Luminous."

He finally let her reclaim her hand and she held it to her cheek, momentarily stunned by his reaction—or lack of it. "Congratulations?" she repeated.

"Sure."

"You're not...upset?"

"Disappointed perhaps, but upset, no. Why? Should I be?"

"Well, no. I mean, I thought you might be. You always said you never wanted children.'' Relief flooded her overloaded emotional system and she babbled on, almost oblivious to his increasingly astounded eyes. "I thought you'd be shocked, that you'd think I had purposely let myself get pregnant. Let me assure you I didn't. It was all a mistake, but now that it's happened, now that I'm used to the idea and have felt the baby kick and the nausea isn't so constant...well, now I'm happy about it. Excited. In awe..."

"I—"

"No, let me finish." Biting her lip, attempting to put the past behind them, she added, "Whatever you and I had together died the night I discovered your marriage proposal was just part of an elaborate scheme. I'm not here to discuss the other women, I'm not here for more accusations. That's in the past. *We're* in the past. I'm not trying to get you to marry me. I wouldn't, even if you asked again, even if you meant it this time.''

She stopped for a breath, her mind racing, wondering if that last part was true, hoping it was, afraid it wasn't. For months, in her mind, she'd downplayed her attraction to him, and now here it was again, stronger than ever, scary and forbidden. She had to keep her head. The stakes were too high to fall back into temptation. She was thinking for two....

"You know my dad left me a little money," she continued before he could interrupt. "If I'm careful, it should last me and the baby for a couple of years. I'm moving back to Nevada so my aunt and uncle can help. When I saw your mom yesterday, I realized I couldn't leave without telling you about this, Ryder.''

She took a deep breath. Her hands were shaking.

He looked as though she'd finally made sense and she momentarily wondered what part of her disclosure had pierced his slick veneer. Actually, considering his disposition, it was something of a miracle that he was still standing there, that he hadn't bolted.

"Are you finished?"

"Well...yes. Yes, I'm finished."

He stared directly into her eyes, projecting a laser-like beam that seemed to melt everything in the path between her irises and her heart. He said, "I can see how hard this...revelation...was for you to make. I hate to have to tell you this, but I'm not Ryder."

For a second, his declaration was like mud slung at a brick wall. Amelia stood transfixed, staring, unbelieving, and then it hit her. Memories came racing back, pictures on top of the television, family stories told by Mrs. Hogan of twins, one of whom Amelia had never met. Ryder's brother, the one who practiced law in California...

"Oh my God. You're Rob," she said woodenly.

He touched her arm. "If it's any help, I'm delighted I'm going to be an uncle. I know I'll be very good at it."

"I can't believe this. I've confessed to the wrong man!"

He nodded. For a moment, she wondered if Ryder was playing some elaborate ruse, but now that she reviewed this man's reactions, she could see that he might look like Ryder, but he didn't act like Ryder.

So what explained that intense sensual burst that had occurred between them? Had he felt it, too, or was it all in her head, a product of knowing she'd been intimate with him? Except she hadn't. He wasn't Ryder.

His voice gentle, he said, "What's your name?"

"Amelia. Amelia Enderling."

He offered her his hand and she realized he wanted to shake, as though this blundering encounter had been a formal introduction. The situation was so absurd and so embarrassing that all she wanted to do was vanish.

After they shook, he said, "I'm sorry I'm not Ryder."

She rubbed her temples with fingers that were still trembling. "I can't imagine anyone being sorry he isn't Ryder," she told him.

This earned her a startled blink. "But you must have…cared…for him once." When her gaze flew to his face, Rob added, "I'm sorry. I just meant that if you're pregnant with his child—"

"I know what you meant," Amelia interrupted. She wanted to add that she'd been with Ryder only once, that she'd been stupid and naive but that would sound as though she was making excuses for herself. She said, "Look, I know he's your brother, a twin brother at that. I don't want to stand here and trash him."

His stare penetrated her. "I'm afraid there's little you could say about my charming brother that I don't already know," he finally said.

She nodded. Her hands fluttered near the life contained within her body and she added, "Merciful heavens, I'm going to have to do this whole thing over again."

Looking over her head, he said, "Sooner than you think."

Amelia turned to face the man she'd really come to address, Rob's twin brother, Ryder.

Ryder. The father of her child. Ryder, with the same smile as his brother, the same flash in his eyes, the same midnight hair and refined features.

"Well, well," Ryder said, his voice slightly slurred. Obviously, he'd been drinking. "Amelia? What are you doing here? I didn't know you knew Rob."

Standing nose to nose, the resemblance between the two brothers was absolutely incredible, from the cut of their hair to the way they walked and the sound of their voices. Only the fraternity ring on Ryder's hand and their boutonnieres differed, Rob's white, Ryder's red. They eyed each other with suspicion and hostility which hinted at a lifetime of turmoil that went a long way toward explaining why Ryder had hardly ever talked about Rob.

"We just met," Amelia said.

Ryder grinned as he said, "You two looked awfully cozy."

"Knock it off," Rob said.

"I came to see you," Amelia said, glancing up at Ryder's face.

Ryder unpinned the red rose from his lapel and drew it across Amelia's cheek. His eyes, so like Rob's, were full of feigned innocence. She knew they belied a fair-weather man who wasn't interested in the long haul. He said, "Well, now, Amelia, I'm glad to see you've come to your senses."

She narrowed her eyes as she brushed the rose away. "My senses?"

"About our little misunderstanding last March."

"Oh," she said, her insides churning. "You mean the 'misunderstanding' we had when you asked me to marry you and then within a week slept with someone else."

"Is that how you remember it?"

"That's how it was," she said.

"Funny, but I don't remember it that way at all," he continued. "Seems to me that you were the anxious one. Not that I minded, I assure you."

Rob formed a fist which Amelia caught on the upswing and held. Though she felt the embarrassing sting of Ryder's words clear down into the center of her heart, she knew that now wasn't the time to acknowledge it. When

Rob finally looked down at her, she said, "Please, let it go."

As Rob slowly lowered his arm, Ryder hooked a flute of champagne from a passing waiter and toasted Amelia. "Here's to you. Here's to last March and all the Marches yet to come."

Rob and Amelia exchanged a quick look. His eyes seemed to say, There's your opening, go for it.

It was cruel that she should have to make this big confession twice in the same afternoon. Either the tension or her pregnancy or a combination of both made her feel wobbly. With a dreadful feeling of déjà vu, she looked at Ryder and said, "There's something I have to tell you."

She felt Rob try to disengage his hand, no doubt so he could beat a hasty retreat. However, as his hand was the only thing keeping Amelia on her feet, she held on tight.

Ryder drained his glass and called out to the waiter who was making another pass with the champagne. "Over here. Just leave the tray."

"Sir—"

"Just leave the tray!" Ryder snapped in his courtroom voice.

As the waiter skittered off without his tray, Amelia took a deep breath and announced, "I might just as well say it, Ryder. I'm pregnant, and you're the father."

There was a long moment of silence that seemed to encompass the whole town of Seaport, maybe the entire state of Oregon. The only realities to Amelia were the feel of Rob's hand and the look of stunned disbelief on Ryder's face. Then Ryder dropped the flute. Heedless of the shards of glass at his feet and the puddle of fizzing wine on the toe of his shoe, he sputtered, "This is a joke, right?"

"It's not a joke," Rob said.

Ryder stabbed a finger in the air at his brother. "*You* keep out of this!"

"Then you calm down."

"It's not a joke," Amelia said.

Ryder stared at her, shaking his head, speechless. She found herself wishing she'd found a better way to tell him, a way that would have given him a chance to assimilate the news without anyone watching.

Quietly, calmly, she repeated her plans, stressing that she wasn't asking for a marriage proposal. She had a feeling he would assume she was trying to put some kind of squeeze on him because that was the way his mind worked. Maybe in his line of work, where people tended to reinvent the past to suit their purpose, it was only natural. None of her explanations seemed to sink in, though. He just kept shaking his head.

"I felt you had to know," she said, "so you can decide what part you want to have in your child's life. You have to tell your folks they're going to be grandparents."

"I don't have to do anything," Ryder said firmly. He looked over her head for a moment, then back, his eyes suddenly cold and calculating. "I know what you're trying to do," he said. "You're trying to use my family to trap me. I'm warning you right now...it won't work."

Rob took a step forward. "Ryder, just listen to her."

Ryder pushed his brother's arm away and gulped more champagne. Amelia wanted to tell him that drinking wasn't going to help, but she suddenly felt a burning desire to escape. She said, "Whether or not you want to be part of your child's life is up to you, Ryder, but I can't believe you would deprive your parents of knowing their first grandchild. Tell them. It's the only decent thing to

do.'' With an apologetic glance at Rob, she released his
hand and escaped the Hogan twins.

The tears started in the ladies' room and continued for
five minutes. After Amelia finally stopped crying, she
became violently ill and lost every bite of lunch. By the
time she'd mopped up her face and washed out her
mouth, almost a half hour had passed. Her only desire
now was to get out of the building without encountering
Nina and Jack Hogan, Ryder's parents. With any luck at
all, they would never even know she'd been there.

Long ago, she'd decided to protect them from the Ryder she knew. Sometimes she wondered how they could
have raised him and not understood what a manipulator
he was. She'd taken the heat for their breakup, blaming
a change of mind, hiding the fact that Ryder had slept
with her after a phony marriage proposal and then
blithely skipped off to the bed of another woman. It was
too late now to change game plans, especially at their
eldest son's wedding.

Besides, she knew Jack Hogan's heart condition was
serious and she wouldn't dream of doing anything that
might make it worse. She loved Nina and Jack—it was
that simple, and that hard.

She was unlocking the door of her car when a commotion at the front of the country club caught her attention.

"Ryder, don't be a fool. You can't drive in your condition,'' Rob said as he tried to keep Ryder from entering
a red sports car pulled up to the curb.

"Mind your own damn business!'' Ryder snarled.

"You haven't changed a bit since college, you know
that?''

Ryder held up his fists. "You want to put your muscle where your mouth is?"

"This isn't the time or place for these kind of antics," Rob said. "Use your head. Philip just got married."

Ryder shoved Rob's shoulder so hard that Rob stumbled backward. Ryder said, "What's wrong, brother? Chicken?"

Rob, apparently pushed to his limit, tore off his jacket and threw it on the grass. Ryder did the same. As the two of them squared off, Amelia murmured a silent apology to her unborn child. Some gene pool she'd chosen.

Before a punch was delivered, Ryder did a quick double step, and with his usual cunning and agility, bolted back to the car and got behind the wheel. Amelia watched as Rob sprinted to the passenger door and tore it open, still arguing with his belligerent brother, begging him not to drive. The engine started with a roar, the car lurched forward, and Rob flung himself into the empty seat.

The car barreled past Amelia who was stunned speechless and motionless at what she'd witnessed. Neither man seemed to notice her, but she would never forget the sight of the two of them, father and uncle-to-be, speeding away from the country club, away from her, away from her child.

Amelia spent the night on the sofa, encased in a sleeping bag. It was her last night in the apartment she had rented furnished for the past three years, and as the morning light stole into the room via the big window over the table, she looked around. The place seemed bare and lonely without her personal belongings, most of which she'd packed in the car the day before. All that remained to be done was to roll up her sleeping bag and throw a few last-minute items into a suitcase.

She snuggled deeper in the folds of flannel, reluctant to get up and begin the long drive to Nevada. She hadn't been back since burying her father the year before. But now that her student teaching job was over and she'd earned her teaching certificate, it seemed the most natural thing in the world to return to her dad's old house and have her baby with her favorite aunt and uncle to help. This was not how she had dreamed of starting a family, but she was determined to make the best of the situation.

A little kick deep within her body brought a smile to Amelia's lips and an overwhelming feeling of contentment. The pregnancy was unplanned, sure, but that didn't mean the baby was unwanted. "Kick away, little one," she murmured. The baby complied.

For an instant, Amelia thought about Rob and the disturbing physical reaction she'd had to a man who turned out to be a virtual stranger. That was the way it had started with Ryder, too. She'd met him after her father died and she needed legal advice. Later she learned that Ryder was an up-and-coming star at his firm, way too hot to handle her measly problems, but he was pinch-hitting that day for a co-worker. At first, she'd thought it was fate that threw them together.

In the beginning, he had seemed like the answer to her prayers—he'd been warm, kind, loving. It took far too long to realize that his behavior was self-serving.

Underneath the good looks and the compassionate words, down in his core, was Rob like Ryder? Did he start out irresistible and slowly turn selfish?

What did it matter? In a couple of days, she would be miles away. Ryder was history...and Rob? No doubt he was another smooth-talking Hogan intent on looking out for number one.

As she tried unsuccessfully to button slacks that had

fit a few days before and were now too tight in the waist, the phone rang. For several seconds, she stared at it in surprise. She'd been under the impression the phone service had been turned off the night before. She could think of no one she wanted to talk to, but the darn thing was persistent.

"Thank God you're home," Nina Hogan's voice cried.

Amelia slid a hand through her shaggy, blond hair, brushing the long bangs off her face. As much as she cared for Nina, she didn't want to talk to her, not now, not until Ryder had had a chance to do it himself. Or maybe he already had! Maybe that was why Nina's voice sounded so distraught.

Amelia steeled herself. "I'm sorry, I was just leaving—"

"You've got to come, Amelia. Say you'll come."

Amelia felt a stir of alarm. "Come where, Nina? What's wrong?"

"We're at the hospital."

Amelia's first thought was of Ryder's dad. She sank down on a kitchen chair. "Is it Jack? Is it his heart?"

"No," Nina cried. "Oh, Amelia, it's Ryder. He's been in a terrible automobile accident. Please say you'll come—"

Amelia found she was standing again. She mumbled, "Ryder?"

"I saw you and him talking at the reception. I know you two were trying to patch things up."

"Well, Nina, actually—"

But Nina interrupted with a swallowed sob. "Philip is off on his honeymoon, and Jack looks so awful he's scaring me half to death. I don't know who else to call—"

"Where's Rob?" Amelia said automatically, though she was already shrugging on her blouse and searching the room with her eyes for her purse. Of course, she'd go, if not for Ryder, then for Nina and Jack.

Nina gasped. "Oh, Amelia, that's…that's the worst part. Ryder and Rob left the reception together. Ryder was driving…there was an accident way out of town…the car ended up in a ravine and no one found them for hours and hours and even then no one could figure out who they were because neither one of them had his wallet. They took the boys to a small clinic while they traced the car back to Ryder's firm. Ryder is unconscious but his brother…our Robby…oh, dear God in heaven, Amelia, Rob is dead."

Amelia stood, stunned, frozen. The image of Ryder and Rob speeding away from the reception together was so clear in her head that she could almost reach out and touch it.

And then a profound ache pierced her heart. Ryder was badly hurt. Rob was dead.

"I'm on my way," she whispered.

"Good Samaritan Hospital. ICU. Hurry."

"I'm on my way."

Chapter Two

The hospital corridor was long and straight. In her haste, Amelia had run across the grass outside, grass which was wet from a sprinkler, and now the soles of her shoes squeaked against the spotless linoleum. She stopped at the nurses' desk to ask the way to the ICU, but before she could form the question, she caught sight of Jack Hogan leaning against a wall at the far end of the hallway. She started toward him.

He looked up when she was within twenty feet. Amelia's pace faltered; the change in Jack's appearance from a few weeks before when she'd bumped into him at the grocery store just about broke her heart.

He was tall like his sons, but stooped today, his skin, always pale, now waxen and dull. He stared at her with the brown eyes he'd passed along to his children, eyes he might very well have passed down to the child Amelia carried inside her. Those eyes were now blurred by unshed tears.

She took his hands and they stared at each other without speaking. His grief was so tangible, it seemed to seep through her skin. She was afraid to ask about Ryder. After a long pause, she finally whispered, "I'm so sorry about Rob."

He nodded as the tears rolled down the creases in his cheeks. She cried along with him.

Nina came through the opaque glass doors, closing them quietly behind her. When she saw Amelia, her composure cracked. "I knew you'd come!" she sobbed as she threw her slight frame into Amelia's arms.

Amelia mumbled, "Ryder. Is he..."

Nina pushed herself away and regarded Amelia with red-rimmed eyes. Her salt and pepper curls looked wilted, defeated, and her mouth was a trembling line of sorrow as she whispered, "He's still in a coma."

"He'll be okay," Amelia said with as much confidence as she could muster.

Nina bit at her lip. "The doctor says he'll come out of it, but she doesn't know when. You'll stay here with him, won't you? I already cleared it with the nurses. They say a fiancée is the same as family. I know having you by his side will make all the difference in the world."

Gently, Amelia said, "But we're not engaged anymore—"

"I know you were only engaged a few days before you broke it off," Nina said, "but I also know you two will work things out."

Amelia searched for a diplomatic way to say that she would stay out in the hall with Nina and Jack for as long as they needed or wanted her to, only please, not in Ryder's room. She kept hearing him say that she was using his family to trap him, and she knew her presence in the room would accomplish nothing. Maybe she should tell them the truth....

But Nina opened her hand just then. Nestled in her palm, like a treasure, was the red rose boutonniere Amelia had last seen when Ryder swept it across her cheek.

"They found it in Ryder's pocket," Nina said, new tears filling her eyes. "Oh, dear God, I don't know what we'll do if we lose him, too."

As Jack comforted his wife, Amelia stared at the bruised flower which had dropped to the floor. In some fuzzy way, it loomed like a sign of her complicity in this tragedy. If only she'd waited to tell Ryder about the baby in private, without alcohol around, how different things might now be.

She knew she would do what Nina and Jack wanted until Ryder awoke and asked her to do differently.

And inside her heart, she, too, mourned for Rob.

He opened his eyes slowly. His lips felt dry. One shaky hand touched the left side of his face. Rough gauze—a bandage?

Where am I?

The room was white, spare, clean...a hospital room. An IV dripped into his arm. The drapes were open and gray skies showed through the glass. Pain throbbed in his temples.

He'd been awake, briefly, once before. Half awake, half a man.

Questions filled his head like loud music, reverberating off the empty spaces in his skull. He felt cold beads of sweat pop out on his forehead and he groaned.

Cool hands touched his arm, and he turned to find a woman staring down at him with eyes as gray as the sky outside.

"It's okay, Ryder," she said softly. "You're going to be fine."

He licked his lips.

"Do you want a drink?"

He managed to nod. She gently held the back of his head as he took a sip of water from the glass she offered. He had seen her once before, when he woke the first time. She'd been asleep in the chair beside his bed then, her chin tilted toward her chest. With a jolt, he realized she must know him which meant he should know her.

But he didn't. He'd never seen her before. Never.

She was quite lovely. Her skin was fine-textured and smooth, her eyes huge, her nose and mouth delicate. Honey-blond hair that looked as though she'd raked it with her hand a dozen times capped her head. She was wearing a roomy, dark blue shirt, the neck open, the sleeves rolled up...a man's shirt that did nothing to detract from her bounding femininity. He was positive she wasn't a nurse. He was just as positive that she wasn't the kind of woman he would forget.

"I'm going to go find your folks," she said.

His folks. Panic began to creep into his brain. He had no memory of parents. He swallowed his heart.

She frowned at him, biting her lip. Then she said, "Don't worry, Ryder, I won't come back now that you're okay."

He caught her hand as she turned away, managing to force out a single word. "Stay."

Her eyes shifted uneasily, but at last she nodded. As his eyelids closed, he concentrated on the feel of her hand in his, the warmth of human flesh in a sea of bleached cotton, a link to the world that was quickly slipping away from him again.

Who was Ryder?

Amelia stood with her hand clasped in Ryder's hand. As far as she knew, this was the first time he'd opened his eyes in three long weeks, and she was dying to call the doctor, to run out into the hall and find Jack and Nina and share the good news.

She didn't move. There was an implied trust in her agreeing to stay and she wouldn't break it. Nor could she force herself to release his hand. Hooking the leg of the chair with a toe, she dragged it closer and perched on the edge.

This was crazy. She needed to alert people. And she needed to prepare herself for Ryder's true awakening when he was clear-headed enough to realize he didn't want to rely on her of all people.

And yet she stayed. For weeks she'd been sitting by this bed, spelling Jack and Nina and Philip after he returned from his honeymoon. She'd been here when they attended Rob's funeral and when they dragged themselves home to try to sleep. She'd been here on days when the sun shined in the window and days when the rain outside echoed the sadness inside. And all the while, she'd told herself she would vanish the second Ryder opened his eyes, that she was anxious to get on the road and set up house in Nevada, to get ready for her baby, that she was here only to help his family.

Now she realized that was only a partial truth. She was here for herself as well, for herself and for their baby. Just the night before, hoping to give Nina and Jack a ray of hope to cling to and knowing it was a miracle her condition had gone unnoticed this long, she had confided that she was carrying Ryder's child. Her news had been met with unqualified joy.

Had she done the right thing in telling them? Should she have kept it to herself? Had she told them because she was afraid Ryder would never wake up and claim his child? And now that the worst was seemingly over and it was time for her to leave, would it break their hearts?

Well, soon Ryder would discover what she'd done and he would feel that she'd backed him into a corner, just as he'd predicted she would.

And yet, she stayed, his hand loosely wrapped around her own. His summer tan had faded at an accelerated rate in the hospital, but she could still discern the faint whitish line across his ring finger. She leaned over and kissed his hand, not realizing until her lips touched his skin what a foolish act it was.

But she had loved him once and he needed her now and he'd asked her to stay. Why?

The door creaked and she turned her head as a stranger entered the room. He was a tall man in his late forties with a graying flattop and piercing black eyes. He wore a charcoal suit over his lanky frame and black shoes that needed polishing. The smile he gave Amelia looked forced and anything but friendly. There was an unmistakable air of officialdom about him.

"May I help you?" she asked, thinking he must have entered the wrong room.

"I'm looking for Ryder T. Hogan," he said, his voice raspy. Gesturing at Ryder like he was a slab of meat, he added, "That him?"

Unexpectedly, Amelia felt a surge of protective ardor. She positioned herself between the man and Ryder. "May I ask who you are?"

He flipped aside his jacket. Fastened to the pocket on his pants was a metal badge. "Detective Hill," he said. "Seaport Police."

"Ryder has been in a coma for two weeks," she said, deciding on the spot to omit mentioning the fact that he'd been awake less than five minutes before. "Obviously, he can't talk to you or anyone else."

"I'm investigating the death of Robert Hogan," he said sternly. "I have questions that need answering."

She felt a piercing stab of fear burn its way through the lining of her stomach. She'd been waiting for this, she realized with a start. Ever since the accident, she'd been anticipating police involvement. Surely blood tests had been taken at the clinic where the brothers were taken after the accident. Surely the results of those blood tests would show that Ryder had been intoxicated.

"When he wakes up, we'll call you," she said. Her voice sounded shaky and her knees felt wobbly. Why didn't he leave? She added, "If you don't believe me, ask his doctors. They'll tell you he's in no shape to talk to anyone."

"I spoke with his doctors," he said. "I wanted to see for myself."

"And now you've seen," she said, praying that Ryder wouldn't choose that minute to open his eyes again.

The detective looked at her closely. She had the feeling there were few secrets kept from his prying gaze and she could feel the heat suffuse her cheeks as she fought to keep hers. He finally said, "Who are you?"

"Amelia Enderling. I'm...I'm Ryder's fiancée."

He nodded as though he'd heard her name before. "Aren't you more of an ex-fiancée?"

"Where did you hear that?"

Glancing at Ryder's still face, he said, "I've talked to some of his friends."

"We made up. I guess his friends don't know about it."

"I guess not. Well, Miss Enderling, are you aware that

your boyfriend had been drinking when he took off with his brother on the night of the…accident?''

There was a telling pause before the word "accident" that sent a chill through Amelia. She bit her lip and kept silent.

"It's common knowledge," he added.

She squared her shoulders. Her initial mistrust of him was becoming more and more pronounced. She finally said, "If you insist on holding a conversation despite what I've told you, maybe we should go out in the hall."

"Why?" he said, a smug smile lifting one corner of his mouth. "He's in a coma, right? He can't hear us."

"How do you know what he can or can't hear?" she snapped. "Just because he's in a coma doesn't mean he's not aware of his environment. Numerous studies have proved—"

Hill interrupted. "It's not you I want to talk to, it's him."

She remained silent.

"I'll check back in a couple of days," he said at last, delivering the message like a warning.

Amelia sank down on the chair as the door closed behind Detective Hill, and she looked at Ryder's face, so recently familiar again.

What would happen to him when he discovered he was responsible for his brother's death and that the police wanted to talk with him about it? The guilt alone would be devastating, for she earnestly believed that beneath Ryder's selfishness was a decent core struggling to get out. And if he was convicted, there would go his life as he knew it.

It wasn't her problem. He would neither expect or desire her involvement, but in his current vulnerable state, it was hard to feel callous. And, too, there was Nina and

Jack to consider—they'd lost Rob because Ryder had been irresponsible and reckless. What would happen if they now lost Ryder to the legal system?

Rob. His death conjured so many emotions. Guilt that she'd told Ryder the big news about the baby when he had access to both liquor and a car. Anger that Ryder had survived a crash he was responsible for. More guilt for the anger because Ryder had not escaped without injury himself. And added to the mix, sadness that Rob, or at least what little she had known of him, would never be the uncle her baby needed, that she would never open the door and find him standing there with a stuffed bear in his arms.

A noise at the door cut short her painful musings. She turned, expecting another go-round with Hill. Instead, she found herself facing Jack and Nina Hogan.

"Thank goodness you're here," she said with relief.

Nina crossed the room quickly, pausing to pat Amelia on the shoulder. "How's our little mother feeling?" she asked, the thrill of Amelia's pregnancy still lighting her eyes.

"Just fine." On the spur of the moment, Amelia decided to delay mentioning the police. Instead, she would share the good news.

Watching their faces closely, she said, "He woke up."

Both of them stared at her as though she'd just delivered a statement in Swahili. "Ryder opened his eyes," she elaborated. "He spoke to me!"

Nina clasped her hands together and squealed.

"What did he say?" Jack demanded.

"Not much. He seemed...confused." At their furrowed expressions, she added, "He was only awake for a minute or two."

"Do the doctors know?"

"I haven't had a chance to tell anyone but you two."

Jack nodded briskly and went back out into the hall, presumably to alert the medical staff. Nina crossed to Ryder's other side and smoothed a lock of dark hair back from his forehead before kissing him.

Amelia looked down at her hands. It was time to leave. She had rehearsed the way she would explain her departure, but now that the time had come, her mouth felt dry and the words were gone.

Jack burst back into the room, Dr. Solomon in tow. She was a middle-aged woman with kinky gray hair and kind eyes. A pair of glasses bobbed on a chain against her ample chest. Amelia had met her on numerous occasions and liked her.

"He was conscious?" the doctor asked as she took Amelia's place by the head of the bed.

"Yes. I gave him a sip of water."

Dr. Solomon shined a small flashlight into Ryder's eyes and called his name softly. Amelia was startled to see Ryder's lids flutter open.

The doctor looked up at Jack and Nina and smiled. Then she looked back at Ryder who was gazing at her with a puzzled expression on his face. "How are you feeling, Ryder?"

He licked his lips. "My head aches," he murmured at last.

"Understandable. You have a concussion. You're doing fine," she said, adding as she stepped out of the way, "there are some people here who want to see you, young man."

Nina, all smiles, said, "Hello, darling."

Ryder's baffled expression deepened. Slowly, he looked from his mother to his father, who stood beaming at the end of the bed, and then to Amelia. When he saw her, he said, "You..."

Amelia heard it as an accusation. She took a step back, toward the door. She'd been expecting this, but now that it was upon her, she felt awkward and embarrassed.

He smiled at her. It was the smile she had loved first, the smile that lit his brown eyes and warmed the room. It also stopped her in her tracks. He said, "You, I know."

"Of course—"

"You were here earlier."

"Yes."

He nodded, wincing slightly as though the motion caused him discomfort. His gaze traveled back to Nina and then to Jack. "I don't know you people," he said.

Jack chuckled. "That's my boy, always with the jokes."

But Nina leaned closer and stared right into her son's eyes. Then she looked over her shoulder at her husband and said, "I don't think Ryder is making a joke."

The doctor said, "These are your parents. Are you saying you don't know them?"

Licking his lips again, Ryder said, "The girl was here earlier when I woke up, but I've never seen any of the rest of you before in my life."

Nina's hands flew to cover her mouth and she gasped. The doctor said, "Do you know who you are?"

He stared hard at her. Amelia could see him trying to search his mind for answers. He finally said, "You keep calling me Ryder. I'm afraid the name doesn't ring a bell."

Jack's face was as bleached as the sheets. He finally said, "You don't know who I am, son?"

Ryder looked contrite as he murmured, "No, I'm

sorry, I don't.'' He struggled to sit up a little in the bed. The doctor helped him with pillows.

"Do you remember the car accident that sent you here in the first place?'' she asked gently.

Again he seemed to search his memory bank which apparently he found empty. Narrowing his eyes, his fists clenched, he finally said, "Damn it, doctor, I don't remember a thing. Not a thing.''

"Calm down,'' she cautioned. "It's not unusual for a head injury to cause temporary amnesia.''

"Amnesia,'' Jack mumbled.

Nina, her hands crossed on her chest as though trying to keep her heart in place, said, "You remember nothing about the accident, Ryder? Nothing?''

The doctor flashed her a warning glance. Nina's gaze shifted to Amelia. Her expression seemed to say, He doesn't remember his own brother! What now? Haven't we been through enough?

Amelia grabbed hold of the one hopeful word and said it out loud. "Temporary?''

"Almost certainly,'' the doctor said brightly. "Give him a day or two.'' With another meaningful look directed at all three of them, she added, "And don't swamp him with details of the accident, not now.''

In other words, thought Amelia, don't tell him he was driving drunk and his brother is dead because of it.

Nina blinked a couple of tears from her eyes. "So you're saying that in a couple of days he'll know who we all are? He'll be himself again?''

The doctor answered with a brisk nod. "Meanwhile, I'll send Doctor Bass in to see you.'' She patted Ryder's knee and added, "He's the staff psychologist. You'll like him.''

Ryder nodded. He looked at Amelia and she realized

with a jolt that to him she was a familiar face, even though that familiarity was only hours old. It left her in an odd position. Did she give him the support he was obviously looking for, or did she protect herself from the man he would be in a few days when his memory returned, when he no longer wanted anything to do with her or their baby?

Unsure, she smiled back.

Chapter Three

 Still a little shaky on his feet, he crossed the room and peered into the small mirror above the sink, searching his eyes for some spark of recognition.

Nothing.

He ran a hand through his hair as he studied each of his features. Straight nose, brown eyes, chin. He opened his mouth and found the proper number of teeth, apparently without a single filling. He needed a shave.

He took a step back and stared at his whole face. The odd thing was that other than the bandage on his left cheek and a general disheveled appearance, he looked exactly as he knew he should look. He just couldn't put a name or, more importantly, a past with himself.

He said, "Ryder. Ryder Todd Hogan. Ryder Hogan."

The brown eyes still looked blank, but he'd heard his name said so many times over the past few hours by doctors, nurses, his parents and especially by the beautiful woman he'd found sitting by his bed, that it was beginning to sound familiar.

"My name is Ryder," he said. But who *was* he? He didn't know which foods he liked, what music he listened to, if he had a dog or a parakeet or a goldfish. He wasn't sure where exactly he was, only that it was overcast outside and everyone spoke English. So how come he could place himself in the United States in late summer, judging by the tree foliage outside his window, near the coast if the seagulls weren't lost, but not identify himself or his loved ones?

Obviously, it was time to ask questions and demand answers.

Reviewing what he knew of the people he'd so far met, he decided Amelia was the one to tackle. His parents—and the thought still left him stunned that he could forget the very people who had given him life and raised him—well, they just looked too fragile to quiz. Amelia, on the other hand, seemed strong. Defiant, maybe. Hesitant about him, definitely. But strong.

He found himself curious about her. Who exactly was she to him? Were they lovers? The thought brought a smile to his lips. He fervently hoped they were and would be again. He was finding it hard to take his eyes off her and more often than not, he caught her sliding gazes his way as well. There was something between them, all right, something he was anxious to explore.

He turned as the door opened and a large man with very short gray hair entered the room. "Ah, I see you're awake," he said.

Ryder, who suddenly felt less than half dressed in the hospital garb that opened down the back, pulled the gown close around his body and said, "Do I know you?"

"No, actually, you don't," the man said. He flipped aside his jacket and Ryder found himself staring at a police shield. "I'm Detective Hill. I have a few questions to ask you."

Ryder shook his head and slowly made his way back to the bed. "I have to warn you," he said. "I'm currently in the dark about damn near everything."

"Yes," Hill said. "I hear you're claiming to have amnesia."

Ryder frowned at the man as he pulled the blankets up over his legs. His head still pounded, but generally speaking, he felt pretty good. He said, "Why do you sound so sure I'm faking it?"

The detective smiled. Maybe smiled wasn't the right word. Smirked might have been closer to it. He said, "It just comes at a rather opportunistic time, that's all. I hear you can't remember a thing about the accident."

"That's right," Ryder said, his gut suddenly clenching like an angry fist. He said, "What should I be remembering, Detective Hill?"

"Well, for starters, your brother."

"I've been told I have a brother named Philip. I understand he was off on his honeymoon when the accident occurred. He's away again for a few weeks so I haven't met him yet, but I can't imagine what he has to do with anything."

"I'm talking about your other brother," Hill said. "Your twin. The one who died when the car you were both riding in hit the bottom of the ravine."

As Ryder stared at Hill, his heart seemed to stop beating. A twin? He shook his head, convinced the man was lying. No one had said a word about a twin brother killed in the accident.

But Hill returned his stare with a defiant tilt to his chin. He wasn't lying.

Ryder's heart began beating again, erratically at first

as though it was only half a heart pumping for half a man. A twin. He'd lost a brother and he didn't remember. He raged against the injustice of it. He was repelled and saddened and furious. He felt vulnerable—why hadn't someone warned him?

Hill's gaze was steady and belligerent. For a second, it seemed the detective was looking right into the depths of Ryder's soul. Let him. Let him see what he wanted to see. Ryder had nothing to hide, only himself to discover.

And then Ryder rebelled against the scrutiny and glanced away. He decided he would not show his tumultuous emotions to the controlled, suspicious man in front of him. The ache this newfound loss produced in his heart seemed too private, too raw, too foreign.

"Where are you going with this?" he choked out at last.

He was answered with narrowed eyes and a sentence delivered staccato. "You're either a very good actor or you're telling the truth. You really don't remember."

"Maybe I'm a very good actor who also can't remember a thing," Ryder said. "Your guess is as good as mine when it comes to knowing who or what I am."

The door swung open and Dr. Solomon came into the room, clipboard in hand. She took one look at Hill over the top of her bifocals and said, "I distinctly recall asking you to wait a few days until this boy's memory returns. Do I have to put a guard in front of his door?"

The detective held up both hands. "I was here anyway so I decided to check—"

"I told you he is currently suffering from acute memory loss."

"I wanted to see for myself," Hill said, leveling a stare at Ryder. "Sometimes doctors are taken in by things the police can see right through."

"Sweet talking will get you nowhere," she said dryly. "Now leave."

Hill started to protest, but the doctor was a tough cookie who refused to budge an inch. She took his arm and gently but firmly expelled him from the room. The man's parting words, delivered with an icy calm, were, "I'll be back, Mr. Hogan. You can count on it."

Amelia had apparently been right out in the hall, for she came in immediately.

She closed the door behind her and leaned against it. Her position made her shirt cling to her body, and once he got past the tantalizing curves of her breasts, he was suddenly aware of the bulge in her abdomen. Was she pregnant? If she was, it put a whole new spin on their relationship.

"What did that man say to you?" she demanded.

Ryder looked from Amelia to the doctor and back again. "He told me I lost a twin brother in the accident that landed me in this hospital." The two women exchanged a long look. Ryder said, "It's true, then."

Dr. Solomon nodded.

"And neither one of you thought to tell me. An oversight?"

The doctor said, "Ah, sarcasm."

"I need to know exactly what happened."

Amelia said, "It was a car accident. You survived, Rob didn't."

"Rob," Ryder said, wishing with all his heart that he could recall this brother. "Were we identical?"

"Yes," Amelia said softly.

Looking at the doctor, he said, "Aren't identical twins supposed to have a special bond of some kind? How can he be dead and I can't even remember him?"

Dr. Solomon touched his arm. "Give yourself time,"

she said. "Maybe you should be thankful that, for the moment, you don't have to face the pain this loss will ultimately cost you."

"Thankful," he mused, feeling anything but. Did she have any idea how frightening it was to feel nothing but a giant void inside your head?

The doctor handed him a small paper cup that held a trio of pills. As she poured water into a glass, she added, "You've had more than your share of excitement for today. Go to sleep now. Maybe when you wake up, all your memories will be exactly where you left them."

"That's what Dr. Bass said," Ryder informed her. "Only he had fancier words for it."

"It's a psychologist's job to have fancy words for everything," Dr. Solomon said with a smile.

He downed the pills. Truth of the matter was, he'd had enough of this day, with people staring at him, waiting for him to remember them, waiting for him to remember anything. And, he admitted to himself, Hill had upset him. What was that guy's problem?

A nurse appeared and he spent the next several minutes having his blood pressure checked and his temperature taken. He could live without any more medical attention, too. Eventually, apparently satisfied that he wasn't going to expire in the next few hours, Dr. Solomon patted his blanket-covered leg and left the room with the nurse. Amelia fluffed his pillows. It seemed to Ryder that she was purposefully avoiding looking at him.

He caught her arm as he laid his head back against the cool softness of the pillow. Her skin was very smooth, like satin. He wondered how often he had touched her in the past, and what kind of feelings his touch engendered now. Did the feel of his skin against hers arouse her the way it did him? Judging from the way she stared at his fingers, the answer was a resounding no.

"I have a few questions I was hoping you could answer," he said, still holding on to her hand.

She looked over her shoulder as though hoping help was lurking in the wings. "Such as?"

"Well, to start with, where are we? Specifically, I mean."

"Seaport, Oregon. Good Samaritan Hospital, room 305. You were born in this hospital over twenty-eight years ago."

"What do I do for a living?"

"You're an attorney with Goodman, Todd and Flanders."

Incredulous, he said, "I'm a lawyer?"

"According to Bill Goodman, a very good lawyer. A trial lawyer mostly, though we met when you helped me settle my father's affairs after he died."

He tried to picture himself in a courtroom. He tried to imagine himself defending a murderer, talking to a jury, approaching a judge. He knew lawyers did all that stuff—he simply could not recall himself in the role.

With a lilt to her voice, she said, "Does it bring back memories for you?"

Slowly, he shook his head. "Not a one."

"The roses are from Miles Flanders. He says you're not to worry about the Dalton case. People you work with have been calling."

He could see she was waiting for all this to ring a mental bell, but the thought of practicing law was as foreign as everything else. Tearing his eyes from the vase of yellow roses, he peered at her intently. "Who, exactly, are *you?*"

"Amelia—"

"I know your name. But who are you? Start with who you are to me."

She shrugged. She said, "We're friends."

He raised her hand to his face and kissed her fingers. She smelled like fresh flowers and sunshine, not at all like the hospital. He yearned to pull her into his arms and find out what her mouth tasted like. The expression on her face stopped him from doing it. She was staring at him as though he was mad, crazy! He said, "Friends? Is that all?"

"Ask me about something else," she said firmly, withdrawing her hand. "Or better yet, go to sleep like the doctor ordered."

He decided to temporarily let her off the hook. "Do I have other siblings I can't recall?"

"No. You have just the two brothers." A sharp intake of breath signaled she'd heard her own words. She said, "I'm sorry. You had two brothers, now you have Philip."

"Was I close to...Rob?"

Her eyes immediately sparkled like distant stars. She took a deep breath and hesitated.

"Come on, Amelia. I'm at a distinct disadvantage with everyone around here. Just tell me the truth. Was I close to my twin brother?"

She wiped away the moisture from her eyes, ran a hand through her hair and said, "Not particularly."

"Why?"

"I'm not sure."

"You're copping out on me," he snapped.

She shook her head. For the first time, it occurred to him that she looked drained, both emotionally and physically. He'd been so aware of the unease in her eyes that he hadn't noticed the dark circles under them. She'd been at his side in the hospital each time he awoke, so she'd probably been here off and on since the accident.

He said, "You're pregnant, aren't you?"

She paused a heartbeat before nodding.

Woozy, he rubbed his forehead and closed his eyes for a second. Damn! The pills were kicking in just as things were getting interesting. He said, "Who's the father?"

She loosened his grip on her arm. Her eyes were huge as she stared at him. Finally, she said, "I don't want to talk about it."

"But—"

"Please. Don't ask me again."

He wanted desperately to press her for details, but his eyelids each weighed a ton. As the world grew dark, he searched his mind for something to cling to. All he could find were a pair of gray eyes.

"It's been almost two weeks," Dr. Solomon said. Seated beside her was the psychologist, Dr. Bass, a man in his early fifties with slick black hair and an elegant pencil-thin mustache. He drummed his fingers against a thick file entitled "R. Hogan."

"Which brings us to the conclusion that this amnesia is going to last a little longer than we hoped," Dr. Solomon continued.

Amelia glanced at Jack and Nina who sat next to her at the conference table. They both looked worn to a frazzle. For different reasons, she knew exactly how they felt. Since awakening, Ryder had gravitated to her for support and comfort, and the struggle to remain friendly but aloof was taking its toll.

"Physically, he's doing very well," Dr. Solomon said.

The shrink, as Ryder called Dr. Bass, added, "I believe the amnesia may be the result of the traumatic events surrounding the accident and his brother's death. Survivor's guilt, in other words."

"But we've been so careful to say nothing," Nina said.

"I don't think he even knows he was driving," Jack added.

Amelia said, "He's been asking a lot of very...difficult questions. I've tried to keep the answers positive and upbeat, like you suggested."

Dr. Bass leaned across the table. "Nevertheless, deep inside his subconscious, he knows. The amnesia may be his way of hiding from the truth. I don't want his guilt in this matter discussed until he's had a little more time."

"I've talked to the district attorney," Dr. Solomon said. "I told him about Ryder's condition and he agreed to delay any criminal action until Ryder recalls who he is and what happened that night. Frankly, I happen to know the blood alcohol tests administered to both Hogan boys at the clinic were botched. The nurse drew the blood, but an orderly made a mess of things."

"It's not the first time we've had trouble with that clinic," Dr. Bass said.

"They're small and understaffed and way out in the middle of nowhere. Anyway, I can't see that the state has a leg to stand on. With Ryder's connections, I don't imagine finding competent legal help will be a problem."

"We've already talked to Mr. Flanders," Nina said. "He told us pretty much the same thing you just did. He says everyone at the office knows they're supposed to be quiet about the details."

Dr. Bass said, "Good. What I want next is for you all to take him home. Back to your place, Mr. and Mrs. Hogan, back to the old room he slept in as a child."

Nina groaned.

Jack said, "We moved into a condominium a couple of months ago. We sold the old house. I couldn't keep it up any longer—"

"And, of course, we never dreamed something like this would happen," Nina interrupted.

"That's right," Jack said, rubbing his chin. His voice grew pained as he added, "Rob moved out years ago, right after college. He went to law school in California and that's where he set up a practice after he graduated. He had a house in San Francisco. Ryder went to law school in Oregon, but he hasn't lived at home for five years. He just moved into a new place about a year ago. To tell you the truth, we don't see all that much of him."

"Not since you two broke up," Nina added, looking at Amelia.

"That's right," Jack added. "After that, he pretty much kept to himself."

"He said he was busy," Nina said with mild reproach.

Amelia tried to look contrite. What she wanted to do was shout, Your rotten son dumped me, not the other way around! He was too busy sleeping with anyone in a skirt to visit you. Don't blame me!

Dr. Bass tapped his pencil again. "Then that's where he should return. Maybe it will help jar loose some memories. And you, Mrs. Hogan, had better stay with him for a while."

Amelia was surprised to see Nina look down at her hands, tears filling her eyes. "I can't," she said finally.

Jack said, "Now, honey—"

"No," she stated flatly, looking right into her husband's eyes. Then she looked back at the doctors. "We've put off going to San Francisco to settle Rob's estate for too long as it is. We've made all the arrangements. We leave tomorrow."

"I can go alone," Jack said. "You stay here with Ryder."

She shook her head defiantly, then she looked at Amelia. "I know this is asking a lot, Amelia, but please, could you stay with Ryder for a couple of weeks? If anyone can bring our son's memory back, it's you." She looked at the doctors and added, "Isn't that right? Wouldn't being around the woman he loves, the woman carrying his child, wouldn't that be what's best?"

Amelia said, "Oh, Nina, you have no idea what you're asking—"

"Yes, I do," Nina said with finality.

It was very clear to Amelia that what Nina was trying to say was that she was afraid to let Jack go alone to San Francisco, that if he did, who knew what might happen to him as he faced the heartwrenching task of going through Rob's belongings. Nina was being asked the impossible—to choose between her husband and her son, one of whom was physically failing, and the other who currently didn't know her from Adam. She was telling Amelia that she had made her choice. She was begging Amelia to make that choice tolerable by filling in for her.

Amelia felt caught between the fantasy of the Ryder she had created for his parents and the reality of the real Ryder who would rather never see her again—if he ever remembered how distasteful he had found her only a few days before. Her heart sank at the thought of returning to Ryder's apartment with him. She hadn't been there since the night they'd made love, since the night, she realized with a jolt, that their child had been created.

So, how did she say no to people she loved and was concerned for? And how did she turn her back on her baby's father when he was totally unaware of what a jerk he had been—and undoubtedly would be once more?

How would she look her child in the face if she didn't do right by Ryder?

Relenting yet again, she said, "I can stay for two weeks."

"Splendid!" Dr. Bass said. "Now that I think of it, you're the perfect choice. It's obvious the boy has a real affinity for you. I'll want you to reacquaint him with his past. Show him pictures, take him to favorite haunts, charm him with the story of how you two fell in love. We don't know exactly what will open the door to his memory, so hold nothing back except details about the accident that killed his brother. I'd rather he had a chance to remember those on his own."

"What about our baby?" she asked, unwilling to admit how reluctant she'd been to talk about this issue with Ryder. However, his questions were becoming more and more adamant and she was running out of excuses.

"Tell him the truth," Dr. Bass said.

Jack smiled hopefully, Nina blotted tears with a tissue. Only Dr. Solomon regarded Amelia with a hooded stare that suggested she alone somehow understood how difficult a chore this was going to be.

Amelia said, "I'll do what I can." To herself she added, Two weeks. I can live through anything for two weeks. And then I'll be on my way....

Chapter Four

Ryder spent the drive home trying to remember the buildings they passed, the river they crossed, anything.

"That's where you work," Amelia said, gesturing to a quaint Victorian house in the heart of Seaport's business district. The block was filled with similar old houses, all converted into commercial residences. Ryder saw an insurance agency, a battered women's shelter, an environmental pro-action group, and on the corner, his own law firm of Goodman, Todd and Flanders. Obviously, he had yet to make partner.

And how did he know about making partner?

"You're office is in the front there, on the second floor."

He stared at the gingerbread and the cupolas, all painted shades of respectable beige and trimmed with dependable black. The hedges were neatly trimmed, the lawn manicured. His name hung on a plaque along with five other names.

None of it aroused so much as a flicker of recognition.

Amelia didn't say it, she didn't have to say it. He knew she was constantly wondering if something struck his memory. He muttered, "It doesn't look familiar."

"Maybe your apartment will."

He nodded for her sake. He was beginning to suspect nothing would ever look familiar again and he was shocked to discover he actually missed the hospital. At least there he'd known a few of the nurses and doctors and his room had begun to acquire a sense of past. But out here? Nothing.

He found he lived in a very upscale apartment overlooking the bay. He must be a damn good attorney to afford a place like this, he thought. Insisting on carrying her suitcase—a man has got to have some pride no matter how washed out he feels—he followed Amelia up a single flight of broad stairs.

She opened his apartment with his keys. As he stood in the entry, like a visitor, she crossed the room and pulled open the drapes, flooding the large living area with light.

"Anything?" she asked as she turned.

He shook his head. He discovered he lived in a world of plush opulence, of thick carpets and rich woodwork, of distinguished pieces of furniture. A fine layer of dust showed on the polished surfaces.

For the first time, looking around him, he felt a kind of belonging. He couldn't remember buying the white brocade sofa, but he knew he liked it, and if sent to the store right now, he might very well pick it out again. The same went for the wool area rug, the original watercolor of a harbor scene that hung on the wall, the matching navy blue club chairs, the botanical prints.

He sighed deeply. Amelia stood by the big window, sunlight framing her lithe body, glinting off the highlights in her golden hair. She was wearing black shorts and a white shirt. Her long legs were enticingly bare, her slender feet encased in black sandals composed entirely of thin straps of leather. He found himself speculating about her in a purely masculine way. Since the first time he'd seen her in his hospital room, he'd had fantasies about her.

Memory was a strange thing, he was beginning to realize. While he had no specific recollection of any one woman, he did know he had made love before. The mechanics were in his head, but all the important stuff—the sound of a particular voice crying out his name, the smell of skin and hair, the features of a beloved face—these memories were lost. And they were what he now found himself craving.

But if Amelia had once been his lover, why was she now so standoffish?

He put his mind to the task at hand. He peeked in at his kitchen and found the cupboards modestly stocked with esoteric gourmet items, all more or less edible right out of the can or jar. The stereo cabinet held stacks of CDs. The address book on his desk was filled with entries so he apparently had lots of friends, though a good majority of them seemed to be women. There was a code to the book, he saw, a matter of checks next to names. He had no memory of devising the code and certainly had no clue now as to what it meant, though he could hazard a guess.

A red light flashed on an answering machine, and without thinking how he knew to replay the messages, he pushed the correct button. A throaty voice gushed out a second or two later, begging him to call. He caught Amelia staring at him as he listened to one female entreaty after another. He flicked off the machine.

"Looks as though I'm a popular guy," he said.

She raised her eyebrows.

The main bedroom held a huge bed covered with a downy quilt. Amelia, who had been following him around as he investigated his own home, paused at the open door. When he sat on the edge of the bed, she turned away, a sudden spot of color in each cheek. Was she embarrassed because she had once shared the bed with him, or embarrassed because she wanted to again? He hoped for the latter. He would bet money on the former.

His closet held a huge assortment of suits and sport jackets, cashmere sweaters, shoes and ties and all the rest, everything exceedingly expensive and orderly. None of it meant a thing to him.

Amelia had returned to the living room. He joined her by an antique wine rack well stocked with what appeared to be expensive labels. He picked out one of the bottles, a '79 cabernet. He knew it was a good label, he knew the vintage was excellent, he had no idea how he knew.

She said, "You'd better not drink. Dr. Solomon said to wait a few days because of your head—"

With an impatient wave of his hand he said, "Is this all my life is about?"

She looked perplexed. "What do you mean?"

He put the bottle back in the rack. "My refrigerator is empty except for three bottles of champagne. My closet is full of clothes. I have an address book crammed with women's names, to say nothing of that answering machine, and a wine rack to die for. Think about it, Amelia. Add the stereo, and my life seems to revolve around wine, women and song. Is that all I'm about?"

She bit her lip in an endearing way he was beginning to recognize. He longed to take her into his arms. He longed to establish a connection with her. He was lonely in such a deep-down, basic, gut-wrenching, throbbing way that he didn't know what to do. He did nothing.

Wetting her lips, clearly thinking, she finally said, "Of course not. You're a fine lawyer. You do some pro bono work at that women's shelter we passed. People like you. You like nice things."

"I can see that."

"It must be...amazing...to be dropped into the middle of your life like this," she added. "We're all strangers to you. Your own home is a mystery."

He detected a note of pity in her voice. Pity was the last thing he wanted from her. He said, "Who are you, Amelia? Why are you here?"

"Your parents—"

"Yes, yes, I know my parents had to go to California to settle Rob's affairs. I know Philip is off on another business trip. But they could have hired a nurse or a sitter for me. Why you?"

She shook her head gently.

"You're carrying my baby, aren't you?"

Her gaze met his and fell. She moved toward the window. He followed her, determined to know.

When she stopped and turned, he was right there by her side. She looked up into his eyes and said, "Yes."

"Then why aren't we married?"

She was silent again. He could see her trying to come up with answers he would like, and it irritated him. "Damn it, Amelia, just tell me the truth!"

She said, "The truth, Ryder? Is that what you really want?"

"Yes," he answered without hesitation, but suddenly he was filled with doubt. Was he such a beast that the people close to him were afraid to tell him about himself?

"Okay," she said, "here goes. Yes, I am carrying your

child. We'd broken up before I discovered I was pregnant, almost six months now. The truth, Ryder, is that you don't want me or this baby in your life. As to why I'm here? Good question."

Her voice petered out, and she turned away.

He touched her shoulder. Looking at the lustrous gold strands of her hair, he said, "If I was such a jerk, why did you ever go out with me in the first place?"

She glanced at him over her shoulder. He longed to wipe the moisture from her eyes, but she did it herself with shaky fingers. "You weren't a jerk at the beginning."

"That's good to hear."

She faced him again and seemed to struggle with her words. "My dad had just died and I was…pretty upset. You were sympathetic…and kind. You seemed to know exactly…well, the right things to say and how to say them."

"But that didn't last?"

"No," she said so softly he had to strain to hear her.

"What happened?"

She shrugged and said, "You got what you wanted."

"I got what I wanted. Oh, you mean that we made love and after that—"

"After that, you lost interest."

"That's impossible for me to believe," he said, staring into her incredible eyes. "Are you sure—"

"People like to talk."

"And that means?"

Her glance was quick and furtive. "Later, after we broke up, I started hearing things."

With dread in his heart he said, "What kind of things?"

"I don't want to hurt you, Ryder—"

"What kind of things?"

"That...well, that you ran around. You had a lot of girlfriends at the same time without any of them knowing about the others. You did and said whatever it took to get what you wanted and then you became bored and moved on. Stuff like that."

"Boy, I'm a winner," he told her as he twisted the heavy gold ring on his right hand. It had been given to him when he left the hospital, told it was his. Like everything else, it felt foreign.

"In all fairness, when you were with me, you were great."

"This sounds promising."

"You sent flowers, even a clown with a bouquet of balloons to my classroom. The kids adored it."

"And you?"

"I adored it, too," she whispered. "You were, *you are*, so smart and well-read—"

"Wait. I don't see many books in this room."

"They're all in the spare room, in boxes, on the shelves. You read everything you get your hands on. Fiction, history, poetry, religion, politics, the whole nine yards."

He felt a slight stirring of excitement. Reading was something he could remember. He loved to read. He glanced instinctively in a corner of the room and found a big leather chair with an ottoman, a low table and a good lamp. The perfect spot for reading, a spot he had known was there before he even looked.

There was a book on the table and he picked it up. It was a collection of love poems marked with a cocktail napkin from Pepper's Place. He had no memory of such an establishment.

Amelia said, "Ryder? Are you okay?"

The feeling of familiarity was gone and Ryder shook his head in frustration. He scanned the poem and found the images both vivid and erotic. It made him slightly dizzy when he looked from the words to the woman staring at him with wide eyes. He closed the book and put it back where he found it. He said, "It's nothing."

"I thought for a moment you remembered something—"

"It's nothing!" he snapped.

She bowed her head.

Instantly contrite, he said, "Amelia, I'm sorry. For a second it seemed as though something was familiar. This memory thing is as elusive as a dream."

"Yes," she said.

He swallowed as her gaze came back to his face. He added, "I'm sorry I was such a heel before. I'm sorry I hurt you and used you and conned you."

She said, "It's okay, I got over it."

"It explains why you're so wary of me."

She nodded. She looked as alone as he felt. He wondered how he could make her see that the old Ryder, the man who would do these things, was gone. He said, "You have no idea what it's like hearing this kind of stuff about yourself. I'm not asking for pity here, or even for forgiveness, but as long as we're together, I hope you'll try to see me as the man I am today."

"And not the one you were yesterday, or will be again tomorrow?"

"Do I have to revert? Is it written somewhere?"

"I have no idea."

"I don't either. If there's any rhyme or reason for what's happened, maybe it's that this is my wake-up call, my chance to improve myself."

She looked doubtful. Her hand rested on top of the

bulge in her abdomen for a second in what he suspected was an unconscious gesture, then she said, "I'll honestly try to do as you ask."

"Thank you."

He could see her reassembling her composure, protecting herself...from him. Now he understood the why, but understanding it didn't make him like it.

"Meanwhile, we have our work cut out for us," she said. "Dr. Bass wants you reacquainted with your past, step by step. Your mother gave me old photo albums and made a list of all the places that were important to you as a child. We'll go shopping later and we'll buy the food I know you like. And there's your office...well, where do you want to start?"

He threw caution to the wind and spoke what was truly on his mind. "How about a hug?"

She stared at him for several moments.

He said, "Amelia, you're carrying my child. You just told me I'm going to be a father. For all intents and purposes, I've never even held you." He opened his arms. "Just a hug."

Finally, she stepped close. She reached up and gently touched the scar that was now the only physical remnant of the accident, her fingers cool against his left cheek. Then she put her arms around him, and he held her tightly, his cheek resting on top of her head, his eyes closed. Once again, he had a fleeting sense of belonging, and he knew, somewhere deep inside himself, that the act of holding Amelia Enderling was familiar.

She was beautiful, kind, patient, proud. If he was as bad as she said he was, how could he have attracted a woman like her? Maybe that was what he should concentrate on, maybe that was the part of himself worth salvaging. She'd seen something in him before, maybe she could see it again.

Her heart beat next to his, their baby, existing in the snug warmth of her womb, was between them. He wondered how he could have turned this woman away. He held her tighter.

A few minutes later, after Ryder excused himself to shower, Amelia let herself out onto the balcony and attempted to button her sweater against the late-afternoon chill which swept over the bay. Thwarted by an ever-increasing girth, she gave up and hugged herself for warmth.

"Why am I here?" she muttered, talking to her baby. It was a habit she'd fallen into early on.

She knew the reasons. Indeed, she repeated them to herself on a regular basis, like a chant or a mantra. Help Jack and Nina. Protect Ryder. Help him rediscover himself. Do what you can to save the father of your child.

This isn't going to be easy, she thought suddenly.

Well, she'd known that going in. She'd known she would have to protect herself. Even under normal circumstances, Ryder could be as charming as the situation called for. That was what made him so tricky.

And these were hardly normal circumstances. He'd held her so close, it almost hurt. And for a moment, she'd been transported back in time. There was a dangerous attraction between them—there always had been. But she'd come out the other side of that attraction several months before and she was not—repeat, not—going to get sucked back into it now.

But, oh, the luxury of his embrace! He said he had no memories of having held her. While her own memory was more than able to conjure up any number of times when she'd been swept away by Ryder's strength, today had been a first for her, too. There was a tenderness to him that had been missing before, and when his breath had become tangled in her hair, she had felt a terrifying surge of desire.

Her baby chose that second to wiggle and kick, and she smiled as she ran a hand lightly over her midsection. She counted the weeks still left, glad she had time to get Ryder back on his feet before devoting herself to her child.

What a miracle this baby was. For his or her sake, Amelia had to keep her head on straight. Soon, the two of them would head for Nevada, for dry heat in the summer and snowy winters, for Aunt Jenny and Uncle Lou and the normal life they would all create for her child. That was her reality, the only reality she could afford to contemplate.

This Ryder—this improved version who exuded warmth—he had no relation to reality at all. He needed her, plain and simple. Whether or not he was currently cognizant of the fact, he was an opportunist. He always had been. That was why he was acting the way he was. The moment she stopped believing this was the moment she should get out of town. As long as she kept in mind the fact that she was little more than his anchor, his balance, and that to help him was an act of kindness tempered with necessity, she would be okay.

But it was more than that and she knew it. This Ryder was the Ryder she'd known at the beginning. This was the man she had loved before she found out he was devious, before she discovered he could never—would never—commit to her. Was there really a chance that he would stay like this even after his memory returned?

"Stop it, Amelia," she mumbled.

Two weeks.

The doorbell rang. She waited a second to see if Ryder had finished his shower and would answer it, but when it rang again, she let herself back inside.

Ryder exited the master bedroom just then. He was naked except for a white towel tied around his waist. His paler than usual skin nevertheless encased an impressive physique that included broad shoulders and a rock-solid torso which narrowed to a slim waist. Glistening drops of water clung to the fine dusting of dark hair across his chest. Thanks to the weeks spent in the hospital, he was thinner than he had been the last time she'd seen him unclothed, but the loss of weight had done nothing to diminish his appeal.

"I'll get it," she said, making sure to look at his face. The slight smile toying with his well-formed lips revealed he was aware she'd given him a once-over.

He ruffled his shining wet hair with a hand towel and regarded her with those deep brown eyes. "It's my apartment. I guess I should answer the door," he said.

"Whatever you want."

He walked away from her, his gait the self-assured near-swagger she recalled, his bare feet leaving tracks in the deep pile of the carpet. Amelia shook her head. This was vintage Ryder, walking around half-dressed, totally at ease with his body. She found herself thinking that even if he didn't know who he was, he *was* who he was.

A middle-aged woman with impossibly blue-black curls stood outside the apartment. She was obviously upset, though surprisingly, it seemed to have nothing to do with the state of undress of the man in front of her.

For a fleeting second, Amelia wondered if she was the distressed mother of some girl Ryder had dumped, and she pondered what she should do if the woman hauled off and hit Ryder. Dr. Solomon had given strict orders to protect his head.

"I'm so sorry, Mr. Hogan," the woman said, which pretty well took care of Amelia's worries. Outraged parents didn't apologize before they decked someone.

Ryder held the towel at his waist. "I'm afraid I don't understand—"

"I meant to get here early and run a vacuum across the floors and take off a layer of dust, just like your dear mother asked, but I got so wrapped up in my last job that I completely forgot about you. I've been bypassing your place for so long I guess I just got out of the habit. When I got home and realized what I'd done, I came right over. I know how you hate for me to come here after five o'clock, sir, and I'm truly sorry. If you'd rather I came back tomorrow, just say so and I'll try to work you in first thing in the morning."

Ryder said, "Who *are* you?"

"I'm Ida Mac Cull, your cleaning lady." She tapped the side of her head with a flat palm and added, "Oh, gosh, that's right. You've got amnesia or something, don't you?"

"Or something," Ryder said dryly.

"Then you don't recognize me?" she asked.

"No, I'm sorry—"

"Oh, don't worry about it, sir, I'm nobody. I mean, I'm just a cleaning lady, a forgetful one at that. Oh, maybe I shouldn't have said forgetful, seeing as you've lost your memory and everything. The mister is always telling me I say the wrong thing. I know you think that too, sir, and I really am sorry about the mix-up—"

"It's okay," he assured her.

"But if you've told me once, you've told me a million times not to go buzzing your door after five o'clock. You said you often had lady friends over.'' She looked past Ryder, right at Amelia, and added, ''Just like you do now. Oh, I am sorry—''

''Please,'' Ryder said, patting her arm. ''This is Amelia Enderling. She's staying with me for a while until I get my memory back.''

''Oh, sir, I didn't mean to imply she was one of your...well, you know, not in her condition, sir, if you get my drift. I just meant—''

As Ida Mac Cull seemed on the verge of flustering herself to death, Amelia decided to intercede. ''Mrs. Mac Cull, why don't you come in and do what needs to be done so you don't have to worry about it tomorrow.''

''If Mr. Hogan is sure—''

Ryder gestured her inside. ''Please,'' he said.

Ida bustled past him and went straight to the kitchen. Ryder leaned down and whispered, ''I'll go put on some clothes and we can go out to eat.''

Amelia worked at denying how his warm breath felt as it caressed her cheek. ''Aren't you too tired for that?'' she asked.

''I obviously agitate the daylights out of that poor woman, so let's give her some peace and quiet. Anyway, we have to eat and since I'm sure there are a couple of restaurants on that list of places we're supposed to revisit together, we can kill two birds with one stone.''

He was right. Besides, there wasn't anything in the house to eat and Amelia didn't really feel like shopping. On the other hand, having just recently regained her appetite after weeks of almost constant nausea, she was hungry and she knew exactly where she would take him. ''I'll go change, too.''

He looked her up and down. She was suddenly exceedingly conscious of her baggy shorts and big white shirt, of the too small sweater she'd thrown on before going out on the balcony. He finally said, "I think you look fabulous just as you are."

She narrowed her eyes, searching for his angle.

"Why are you looking at me like that?"

"The old Ryder wouldn't have worried about agitating the cleaning lady, nor would he have been seen in a restaurant with me dressed like this."

"Ah, the old Ryder strikes again."

"I know I promised to try to see you for who you presently are, but sometimes you just surprise me."

"I think you mean that as a compliment."

"I think I do, too," she agreed, and gratefully closed the spare bedroom door behind her, anxious for a second to collect her wits. Apparently, she admitted to herself as she hoisted her suitcase atop a box filled with books and shook out a yellow dress, Mrs. Mac Cull wasn't the only woman Ryder was capable of agitating.

The Mona Lisa was overflowing with a weekend crowd. Nevertheless, a maître d' Amelia recognized from the months she and Ryder dated steadily, met them at the podium with a huge smile of welcome.

"Mr. Hogan," Enrico said, beaming and extending a hand. "It's been too long."

Ryder accepted the enthusiastic handshake with little more than a confused flicker of his eyes. Enrico's gaze slid to Amelia. She could almost see him decide not to mention her obvious pregnancy. Instead he said, "And Miss Enderling, isn't it?"

"You have a remarkable memory, Enrico," she murmured.

"Just for special people," he said smoothly.

"It's crowded tonight," Amelia said.

"Always on a Saturday," he said. Clapping Ryder on the shoulder, he added, "My friend, I heard about your brother. My condolences."

Ryder said, "Thank you."

Enrico nodded curtly. "Now, you and Miss Enderling wait at the bar and I'll see you get a table pronto. And tonight, dinner is on the house. No, no, I insist." He looked over his shoulder, caught the bartender's eye and added, "Kevin, look who's here."

The bartender was a blond man Amelia had never seen before. "The usual?" he asked Ryder, and turning, began to build Ryder's favorite drink, a huge margarita—stirred, not blended. Amelia asked for bottled water with a twist.

Ryder stared at the mixed drink.

"It's what you always have when you come here," she said.

"I like this?"

"Yes."

"And I'm that predictable?"

"Yes," she said. "You always have a margarita and then you order calamari."

"That, at least, sounds right," he said with a weak smile. "I know I love calamari. Do they serve it with an *aioli* sauce?"

"They make the best in town. According to you, anyway."

He took a sip of his drink and made a face.

"Well, you're not supposed to drink alcohol anyway," she reminded him.

Pushing the margarita away, Ryder asked for the same thing Amelia was drinking. Sitting on a bar stool with Ryder behind her, she caught sight of their reflection in the mirror in back of the bar. The crowd seemed to recede and it was as though she was looking at a photograph taken months before. This was the restaurant they had come to on their first date. Then, she'd been super aware of him, nervous about saying the wrong thing, anxious.

She felt exactly the same way tonight.

"Well?" she said, turning to face him.

Her gaze followed his as he looked around. The bar was on the ground floor, the balcony above held dining tables. Steep wooden stairs climbed the wall to their left, an open kitchen occupied the back. The restaurant was noisy with the clatter of plates, the sizzle of cooking, the sound of voices and laughter. It was the kind of place Ryder adored: loud, prosperous, trendy, expensive.

His gaze returned to her face. "Obviously it should jar a memory."

"Yes," she said, nodding.

"But it doesn't."

"Try not to worry about it," she said.

"You have no idea how many things I worry about," he told her. "For instance, I looked in my wallet before we came here. I must have a dozen credit cards. No cash to speak of, just credit cards."

"That sounds about right."

"And no picture of you."

"That doesn't surprise me."

"I'd like one."

She swallowed hard, about to protest, then decided against it. "Sure," she said.

"Why is the restaurant buying us dinner?"

"Because you're one of their best customers. You bring scads of clients for long lunches, and you eat dinner here on a regular basis."

"Did you and I come often?"

"This is where we came on our first date," she said. "And then about once a week after that."

He smiled. "Did I ever kiss you here?"

Amelia paused for a second. "As a matter of fact, you kissed me for the first time right at this bar, right down there."

He looked where she gestured, at the stools several feet away which were now occupied by other people, then back at her. "I wish I could remember," he said so softly his words were almost lost.

For a second, their eyes held, and Amelia felt the old, familiar sensation of drowning. For a second, she wondered what she would do if he closed the distance between them and kissed her. The expectation of this act was so acute, her lips pulsed. Maybe a kiss would help rebuild his memory, she rationalized as she sensed he had the exact same thought she did and was about to claim her mouth.

A ripple of female laughter broke the tension between them. Ryder drew back as a curvaceous blonde wearing a tight, pink dress appeared at his elbow.

"Ryder Hogan!" she said, pouting, her voice loud, her eyes sparkling. "You bad boy, you! Why haven't you called me back?"

"I've—"

"Oh, darlin', I heard all the stories, but I figured it was just your way of standing me up!" The woman's gaze flicked across Amelia, pausing for a heartbeat on her pregnant tummy. With a tilt of her head, she seemed to dismiss Amelia as someone of no consequence, and leaning so close to Ryder her breasts pressed against his arm, whispered loud enough for Amelia to hear, "Party at your place tonight, baby?"

"Ah, not tonight," he said.

The pout deepened, but was ruined with a wink. She took his chin in one hand and peered at his face, turning it so that his left cheek caught the light. With a throaty chuckle, she said, "That scar makes you look sexier than ever, you devil." She punctuated this remark with a kiss on his lips. "You call me, you hear?"

"Yeah," he said, and watched her walk away. "Who was that?" he said after a deep breath.

The moment ruined, Amelia said, "How in the world would I know? You look nice in her lipstick, though. Not all men can wear that shade of pink."

Wiping his mouth with a bar napkin, he said, "She sure seemed to know who I was."

"If you hurry, maybe you can catch up with her. I'm not helping restore your memory very well, maybe she'd have better luck."

"Do I detect a note of jealousy in your voice?"

"You'd love that, wouldn't you?"

"I don't know, would I?"

"Yes," she said firmly. "Yes, you would love it if I were jealous. It wouldn't really mean anything to you, but you'd still enjoy it."

He frowned for a second, then to Amelia's surprise, he grabbed her hand. Before she could question him, he was leading her out of the restaurant. Good grief, was he really going to race after that flirt? If he was, why in the world was he dragging along a pregnant woman!

This was the old Ryder, unpredictable, egocentric, impossible! She said, "Wait—"

He opened the door and propelled them both onto the sidewalk.

Chapter Five

Amelia planted her feet. "Ryder!"

He turned to face her. "What?"

She swallowed words of anger as a stream of people parted to go around them. Ryder grabbed her wrist and pulled her close to the building, out of the way. He looked down at her, his face heavily shadowed, his expression intense.

"I'm going to have to insist that while we're... together, you show me at least a modicum of respect."

His eyes grew large. "Respect!"

Bristling, Amelia straightened her shoulders. "I don't think it's too much to ask—"

"How am I not showing you respect?"

"Chasing after that woman—"

"Chasing? Is that what you think I'm doing?"

"Aren't you?"

"Hell, no!"

She narrowed her eyes. "Then what in the world is going on here, Ryder?"

He guided her away from the front of the restaurant, down the sidewalk, toward the parking lot. Finally, he stopped by a window display of music boxes. After a lengthy pause, he said, "I had to get out of there."

"Why?"

"Think about it, Amelia," he said. "There we are, having a perfectly fine time. I'm rediscovering the joys of the Mona Lisa and looking forward to the calamari, you're finally beginning to relax, when all of a sudden that woman sashays up to me, plants a kiss on my mouth and calls me a sexy devil. All this in front of you."

He looked down at his shoes, then up into her eyes and added, "Then you tell me that in the recent past, I would have liked making you jealous and miserable even though it wouldn't have really mattered to me."

Damn if he didn't manage to sound sincere! Was he? Or was this still the old Ryder, a con artist of exceptional talent? Biting her lip, searching for a way to be kind without falling into the familiar trap entitled fool, she finally said, "I never said I was miserable."

He kind of smiled. "No, I guess you didn't."

"And you didn't seem to mind her...attentions."

"Her attentions?" He scoffed. "Is that what you call it? Did you see the way the bartender winked at me? Can you imagine what it feels like to be with the woman who is carrying your child while another woman comes onto you and everyone around is winking and smiling? It made me feel slimy."

"But that's your favorite haunt, Ryder. And try to remember that you never knew I was pregnant until the afternoon of the accident. Anything you did between our breaking up and the car going off the road didn't have much to do with me.''

"Wait a second. What do you mean? You hid your pregnancy from me?''

"Well—''

"That's supposed to make me feel better?''

"Don't you want to go back inside and have dinner?''

"No,'' he said emphatically.

"But you love the Mona Lisa—''

"Maybe I loved it in the past,'' he said evenly, "but right now, it feels like a shoe that doesn't fit. I think I've lost my appetite. Let's walk around for a while.''

Amelia, trying her best to ignore the gnawing hunger that threatened to engulf her, pasted a smile on her face, a smile that wavered only slightly as she allowed Ryder to take her hand and tuck it beneath his arm.

Ryder lay awake, a distant foghorn sounding a repetitive refrain that echoed the vast emptiness he felt inside his head.

The painkiller Amelia had given him before bed hadn't kicked in yet, which gave him time to relax and think. Trouble was, he had damn near nothing to think about, at least nothing pleasant.

He closed his eyes and formed a picture of himself, then he gave it a name…Rob. A man who looked like him and shared his genes. Ryder knew very few details of the car crash—the doctors had told him they wanted that particular memory to rebuild itself naturally and he should try to be content until that happened.

His twin was dead. A twin he could visualize because of their identical looks, but not one he could mourn properly, not a flesh and blood man. They had been children together. They had undoubtedly laughed together, fought over toys, conspired against friends and teachers and parents. They had chosen the same occupation.

And yet as men they hadn't been close. They'd lived a thousand miles apart. On the other hand, they had apparently shared a love of art and books. And, at the end, at Rob's end, they had been in the same car going to the same place. For the first time, he wondered where that place was. Why had they been out on an old logging road on the evening of Philip's wedding?

His thoughts slid easily to Amelia. He didn't need to rebuild her face. Her image seemed to be permanently engraved in his brain, front and center. For a second in the bar, when he'd gazed deep into her eyes, he'd felt a primal pull toward her. He'd anticipated the moment their lips would touch, and hadn't even dared to take a breath for fear that it would break the spell between them. There had been a huge part of him that yearned to pick her up, sling her over a shoulder, and bring her back here. She was his—he felt this instinctively. That she didn't want to be his was becoming increasingly obvious.

He punched his pillow and resettled himself under the blankets when what he was dying to do was tiptoe to the spare room, thread his way through the maze of boxes, and climb into her bed. Pregnant or not, she was a very sensual, very lovely woman who aroused all sorts of wild thoughts and feelings. So why had he run around on her?

Yawning, the medication finally taking effect, he pushed thoughts of Amelia aside. As tantalizing as speculating about her could be, it was also extremely frustrating. Besides, he had other matters to consider. He was going to be a father. Imagine that! Even if his memory never returned, here at least would be one person whose life would be an open book to him. He was going to make up for his past by being there for his child. And his child's mother.

Amelia would just have to accept it.

Amelia awoke with a headache and a ferocious need for coffee. Hoisting her suitcase on the bed, she rummaged for clothes, pausing when her hand touched the tissue paper nestled near the bottom.

She sat on the edge of the mattress and withdrew the tissue-wrapped item. It was a last-minute baby gift, given to her by her elderly neighbor when the woman realized Amelia was leaving. Amelia unwrapped the tiny white sleeper and held it up in front of her.

Fighting against tears, she thought how amazing, how incredible, it all was. Soon, this soft, little sleeper would encase a real live baby. She lowered the garment in her arms and moved slowly, back and forth, as though rocking it. One tear made it past her defenses and slid down her cheek as she closed her eyes and tried to imagine the tiny garment surrounding something warm and solid and alive.

Her baby. To love, to nurture, to protect.

She was beginning to realize that for a woman, a baby came with a host of dreams. Dreams to make things better, to make things count, to make things good.

Dreams to share.

She folded the sleeper back in the tissue and dug for her own clothes—white shorts, a blue shirt and running shoes. Today was a day for action.

Catching sight of herself in the mirror, she turned to the side, smoothed her blouse down over her rounded belly, smiled, then frowned. The image of the blonde with the hourglass figure wiggled through her mind.

She went to the bathroom and splashed cold water on

her face, brushed her teeth and hair and left it at that. What did it matter to her if Ryder thought she was rotund? All the better.

Part of resisting Ryder's allure, she'd decided as she tossed and turned during the night, was to focus on helping him get well without reacting to him as a man. That meant no lying awake thinking about the fact that he was asleep on the other side of the wall. No imagining his captivating body rolled up in his downy comforter, his black hair stark against the white pillowcase. No romantic musings of creeping into his arms and helping him find his missing memories.

Today they would take a more hands-off, more traditional route to recapturing Ryder's past. Picture albums, visits to schools and the old house in which he'd been raised. Nice, safe stuff.

Ryder's bedroom door was still closed, which probably meant that despite the painkillers, he, too, had had a restless night. She was glad to have the extra time alone.

As she approached the kitchen, she heard the sound of the refrigerator door opening. Ryder was up, after all. That he was fully clothed in slacks and a jacket surprised her, as did the fact that he was holding a dozen eggs in one hand and a cantaloupe in the other.

He looked marvelous in a soft taupe jacket and a shirt a shade darker. The tie he wore, an ivory, brown and moss-green silk affair, had been her Christmas gift to him. He'd barely acknowledged it then, but now he wore it with his usual aplomb and she couldn't help but wonder if deep inside his psyche, he knew it had come from her.

His eyes, as he turned to face her, were piercing. The blonde was right—the scar on his left cheek did make him look sexier than ever.

"Morning," he said.

Amelia finally noticed the shopping bags on the counter. "Good morning. Have you already been to a grocery store?"

"There wasn't any food in the house," he told her as he put eggs and fruit and bread on the counter. "I mean, anything besides canned oysters and caviar. Pregnant women, especially pregnant women who didn't get dinner, need breakfast."

Stunned that he cared one way or another about her dining requirements, she said, "How did you find the store?"

"I walked down to the manager's apartment and asked. She called a taxi for me. The people at the store recognized me. One clerk told me this was the first time she'd ever seen me buy actual food. Apparently, I usually buy beer and wine and snacks. Another clerk offered me a ride home. On the way, she informed me she is one of the female voices on my answering machine."

Amelia leaned against the counter. "You've had quite a morning."

"A laugh a minute."

She spied a small bag of freshly ground coffee—neatly labeled in Ryder's precise hand—and pulled it out. The coffee machine was on the drainboard. Before she knew it, Ryder was standing by her side. "What are you doing?" he asked, his brows knit together.

"I'm going to make a pot of coffee."

"I don't want any, thanks."

"Okay. Then I'll just make enough for me."

"But you're pregnant."

She feigned surprise. "You're kidding? You mean I'm not just getting fat?"

"Ha, ha."

As she scooped the rich ground beans into the filter,

she added, "The doctor said I can have one cup a day. I have that cup every morning. If you could remember, you'd know I don't even start to be human until after the second cup, so this is a huge sacrifice I make for my child."

"For *our* child," he said, glancing down at her abdomen.

She looked up at him as she folded the coffee bag over on itself.

"Our child," he repeated.

"Yes. Our child."

"We need to talk about this."

Amelia felt a flutter in her stomach that had nothing to do with very tiny elbows and knees stretching and kicking, and had everything to do with Ryder's words. She filled a mug with water, poured it in the reservoir, and clicked on the machine. Fortification on the way, she looked up at him again and said, "Exactly what do we need to talk about, Ryder?"

"About how we're going to raise our baby."

There had been a time when she would have killed to hear those words. Now they left her feeling chilled and a little frightened. She wasn't used to sharing the idea of raising this child. Her child. Part of her body, part of her soul. She hadn't even told Ryder that as soon as his folks returned, she was Nevada-bound. He hadn't asked and she hadn't volunteered any information about her plans.

He said, "I've upset you."

"No—"

"You don't lie well," he said.

She shook her head. It had been on the tip of her tongue to say that on the other hand he lied very well, but that was a cheap shot. She said instead, "Let me drink my coffee first, please. Anyway, how do you know too much caffeine can hurt a developing fetus?''

He shrugged. "I haven't the slightest idea. Maybe I read it somewhere."

"Hmm—"

"It's a good thing the store and the cab driver took credit cards because I also don't have the foggiest idea what my ATM number is. Do you?"

"Of course not. But the spare room I'm staying in has a desk in the corner so I imagine your files are in there."

"I'll take a look later. Well, what's on the docket for today?"

"How are you feeling?"

"So good I'll settle for aspirin instead of those knock-out pills."

"Well, we can either look at pictures in an album or we can take a drive around town."

"Definitely the drive."

Amelia poured her one cup of coffee while Ryder stared at the fruit.

"Which do I like?" he asked at last. "Cantaloupe or grapefruit?"

"You like them both," she said.

Since Ryder's car had been totaled in the crash, they took Amelia's car. In light of his questions that morning concerning the raising of the baby, she was glad she'd taken the time to store most of her belongings in a friend's garage. A few boxes were in the trunk, but unless they had a flat Ryder wouldn't see them.

She drove directly to a sprawling grammar school in the middle of Seaport. As it was still August, school hadn't begun yet, so the grounds were more or less deserted.

"Your mother said you went here from kindergarten through sixth grade," she told him.

"It doesn't do a thing for me."

"It's a nice little school. I did my student teaching in that room at the end."

"I bet you're a great teacher."

"Why do you say that?"

He smiled. "You're warm and compassionate and tender, and you have a wry sense of humor. You look like an angel, your voice is soft but firm, and your hair alone is worth a sonnet."

"My," Amelia said, somewhat startled. "Well, I don't know how many five-year-olds go around thinking about sonnets. I hope you're right, though. I hope I'm a good teacher. You wouldn't believe how creative and funny a five- or six-year-old can be. I can't wait to have one of my own."

"It appears you'll have to wait about five years," Ryder said, glancing at her mid-section. He looked at the list and added, "Let's try the Junior High School."

She drove two miles through a maze of streets until they came to a wire fence. They were at the back of the school near the ballpark. A handful of pre-teen boys were getting ready to play a game of baseball.

"I wonder if I ever played here on a summer morning," Ryder said.

Amelia looked at the list. "Your mom wrote down that you played basketball and baseball."

"I'll be right back," he said as he got out of the car. Amelia watched him walk through a gate in the fence and approach the boys. The next thing she knew, he'd taken off his jacket and rolled up his sleeves. One boy handed him a wooden bat, and Ryder took the plate. He swung at a pitch and missed it, swung at another and hit the ball halfway across the field. While the boys hollered, Ryder trotted carefully around the makeshift bases, slapping hands as if he'd just brought home a major-league pennant. Then he spoke with the kids, reclaimed his jacket, and walked back to the car.

He threw his jacket in the back seat and sat down with a deep sigh and an even deeper smile. Something about his expression made her think that he'd remembered who he was.

She was startled to find that she had ambiguous feelings about it. If he remembered being Ryder, then he would also remember how he felt about her. Amelia was hoping that when that day came, she wouldn't be trapped in a small car with him.

And when that day came, she would have to leave and probably never see him again.

The thought jarred her on a couple of levels. She should want to leave—she did want to leave, right?

Maybe.

Maybe not.

If Ryder stayed the way he was…

Amelia felt trapped in a deep pool of confusion.

He said, "That felt good."

Suddenly nervous, she said, "You obviously remember how to hit a ball."

"Yeah. Unfortunately, that's all I remember."

So, the smile had simply been a response to hitting a ball. Was his delight because his subconscious found comfort in something familiar, or because connecting bat and ball was fun?

"What's next?"

Home, she wanted to say. She wanted to give him the keys and let him drive himself around. She was unexpectedly angry with Nina for running out on her son, and with the doctors who had suggested this ridiculous plan of action.

Even as these wayward thoughts skittered through her brain, she knew Ryder's parents and doctors weren't to blame—she was here because she wanted to be here. All she could do was make sure it was for the right reasons.

She said, "Your high school is a couple of miles away. After high school, you and Rob both went to college in Oakdale."

"Where's Oakdale?"

"About an hour east of here. You both earned your undergraduate degrees on the same campus."

"Skip the high school. Let's go look at the college."

Midway between the city limit and the college campus, Amelia recognized a signpost and made an impromptu left turn. "Check the list," she told Ryder. "See if there isn't something about your grandparents' house being on Hillside Road."

Scanning the paper, he said, "Says here 1236 Hillside."

They had to search carefully as the road quickly turned rural and posted addresses became a rarity. Amelia was about to give up when they came to a huge yellow field on the side of a gentle slope. Centered on the field was a small white house. A long straight driveway wandered up one side of a dilapidated fence. The letters on the post were metal and read 1239, but the spacing looked suspicious. Sure enough, when Ryder checked, they discovered the top nail on the six had popped out of the rotten wood and allowed the six to swing down and turn into a nine.

Amelia drove slowly up the rutted drive. It wasn't until they reached the turnaround next to the house that they realized the place was abandoned. Windows were broken or missing. The front door hung on one hinge. Ivy had grown up the chimney and now crept across the decayed shake roof. A rambling pink rose bush had taken over the front porch. Tall grass jutted through gaps in the foundation.

Ryder got out of the car. Amelia wanted to leave him alone with his thoughts, but she'd been sitting too long and needed to stretch her legs. She walked the opposite direction from him, again trying to give him space. They met in the backyard. Ryder looked thoughtful.

"Don't ask me why, but this place feels familiar."

"That's wonderful! Your grandparents lived here until you were ten or eleven," she said.

"Where are they now?"

"Your father told me his parents both died a decade ago. This house belonged to Nina's folks. If I remember correctly, your grandmother passed away over five years ago and your grandfather is still living in a rest home."

"And I can't remember any of them," he said.

Amelia looked at the barbecue in one corner of the yard, claimed now by weeds, stray bricks lying haphazardly on the ground. It didn't take much of an imagination to picture Ryder and Rob and their older brother Philip playing baseball in the field while their grandfather grilled hot dogs. The past seemed so vibrant, it made her skin tingle.

Ryder turned suddenly and looked up the hill and Amelia followed his lead. Amber grass ended at the horizon where it touched an azure sky. The rounded shape of a solitary tree graced the crest. Without a word, he started ambling up the hill toward the tree.

Amelia followed.

Ryder had worn down a swatch of knee-high stalks

and she was able to walk along a fairly manageable path. He disappeared over the knoll. She trudged to the top.

He was standing behind the tree. When he heard her approach, he reached out and took her hand, pulling her to his side.

"There used to be a swing here," he said. He smiled wistfully and pointed at the big branch over their heads. Two decaying ropes could be seen through the foliage. "I don't remember it," he added.

"Then why did you come up here?"

He still had her hand closed in his and it was doing crazy things to all the sensory receptors up and down her arm. It was just a hand, linked with her hand, warm fingers and a strong grip. He seemed distracted by his own thoughts, oblivious to the sublime torture his proximity generated. He was staring down at the bottom of the far side of the hill toward a winding line of green trees.

"I thought there was a river," he said.

How was she supposed to maintain her equilibrium and watch her emotions if he insisted on acting as though it was the most natural thing in the world to touch her? This wasn't fair. She could feel his body beside hers, she could hear his breathing in her right ear. She wanted him to let go of her and yet she felt weak with the hope he wouldn't. She finally said, "Your river is probably down among those trees."

Amazingly, her voice sounded normal and betrayed none of the fluttering indecision that was so rampant in her heart. Her hand still in his, he began strolling down the back of the slope toward the trees.

Amelia meant to pull back and let him go alone, but his quiet determination got the best of her. He moved at a brisk pace, but not too fast. She got the impression he was looking out for her, and sure enough, when the ground became rocky, he stopped and swooped her up into his arms.

He carried her effortlessly, smiling down at her with his earthy eyes, his teeth even and white, his smile enough to die for.

"You can put me down," she said.

He ignored her as he rounded a blackberry patch and entered the shaded belt of trees. Water could be heard now, not rushing, but tinkling, gentle, soothing…the exact opposite of how Amelia felt.

Pressed against his chest, one of his hands on the bare skin behind her knees and the other clutched around her rib cage, she was intolerably aware of the musky fragrance he always wore, of his power. He had always been an enigma to her, animal strength wrapped in modern civilized man. She felt light-headed.

"This all seems familiar," he said at last, and his voice held a rare note of joy that mesmerized Amelia. "I bet you a million bucks there's a rope swing down here and a boulder and a deep pool."

"You don't have a million bucks," she said, staring up at his lips.

"So if I'm wrong, sue me," he said, glancing down at her. His look lingered. Amelia was way too aware of the feel of the back of his neck beneath her hands, the proximity of his face. She blinked a couple of times, and he smiled again, gently returning her feet to the ground.

The river was easily ten feet wide, and just as Ryder predicted, a mound of boulders edged a deep pool. An old rope tied to an overhanging branch dangled above the huge rocks.

He put his weight on the rope. The tree groaned a little, but that was all. Next, he peered into the pool. "I can see the bottom," he said.

Amelia looked over his shoulder. "How deep is it?"

"Only one way to know for sure," he said, taking off his shoes.

"You're not thinking what I think you're thinking, are you?"

"I think I am," he said, peeling off socks.

"The doctor said to watch your head."

He leveled her with an intense stare that once more affected her equilibrium. "You know what, Amelia? Sometimes, the most prudent course of action is to ignore the most prudent course of action."

"In other words?"

"To hell with the doctors."

"If you drown yourself, don't come whining to me."

"Deal."

She found herself a rock to sit on and watched Ryder strip off his slacks and his shirt and his fifty-dollar tie. He wore only sky blue briefs and she tried her best not to stare at him.

"Caught you watching," he said.

"You have always been something of an exhibitionist."

"Really? You see? Piece by piece, I am rediscovering myself."

"Seems to me, you're rediscovering the odd pieces."

"You have to take it as it comes, so says the venerable Dr. Bass as edited by yours truly." He carefully climbed down the rock and maneuvered his way into the pool, whooping as the cool water rose up his legs. Then he quickly dived in.

As he made his way to the bottom to check the depth, she discovered that yes, indeed, the water was clear. She could see muscles rippling in his back and flexing in his powerful legs as he swam. His black hair streamed out behind him, longer wet than when dry. And when he broke the surface, grinning, she felt an answering grin tug at the corners of her mouth.

She tried not to dwell on the insanity of liking this new Ryder. It was bad enough to have loved the old one.

Within seconds, he was back on top of the boulder. Again, she attempted to avert her gaze. Maybe he'd never seen himself dripping wet in his underwear before. Or maybe, more to character, he just didn't care.

Staring at a nearby trail of ants, she said, "Ryder, you've had a concussion. You have amnesia. Do you really think it's smart to risk bashing your head?"

"Probably not," he said, and as she looked up, he grabbed the rope and, yelling, leapt over the edge of the boulder and swung out over the river. There was a second when their eyes met, and then he splashed into the pool. Amelia gasped as drops of water hit her face and bare legs. She got up and looked over the edge, half expecting to find Ryder floating listlessly on the surface, but he was swimming to the shore instead.

If she hadn't been pregnant, she thought, she would join him, bathing suit or no bathing suit.

And that was when she remembered to remember who she was dealing with. All the old reservations came storming back. All the warnings she dutifully delivered to herself on an hourly basis reasserted themselves.

This was a man who was sure she was trying to trap him into marriage. This was a man she couldn't trust.

And she was the wrong person to help him, for his sake as well as hers. It was a conundrum. To get well, he needed to be accepted for who he was at this very moment so he could find out who he used to be. To protect herself and her child, she had to remember at all times exactly who he had been and would be again.

He needed someone to help him who had nothing to lose—no prejudices, no agenda of their own. She should leave. For his sake, as well as her own.

He climbed up on the rock and came to stand in back of her. He said, "Did the old Ryder get...ideas...in his head when he got wet?"

The soft, whispering quality of his voice left no doubt as to what kind of *ideas* he was thinking. She felt shivers tingle her spine and purposely avoided telling him the answer was yes.

He kissed her shoulder. His lips seemed to burn a hole through her cotton blouse. Then he lifted her hair away from her neck and kissed her behind the ear and she felt the sensation clear down to her knees.

Amelia twirled around. Ryder caught her arms to steady her. A shaft of sunlight hit his wet hair and bare shoulders, making them glisten.

And then he was kissing her, his cool, damp lips barely masking a fiery need that seemed to burn beneath the surface. It had been months since she'd kissed him, and she was disturbed to discover that none of the magic was gone. In fact, horror of horrors, it was worse than ever. In the past he had been sexy and thrilling and a little intimidating. Now he was all of those things and more.

Much more.

She pulled away.

He touched her cheek with damp fingers and stared deep into her eyes and she got the distinct feeling that she'd better put an end to this before he got carried away and things between them became even more awkward than they already were. This was the old Ryder, she realized, taking what he wanted, not asking, just taking, and so charming he usually got away with it.

"I don't think you should kiss me again," she said calmly.

"We've kissed before," he said, eyes twinkling.

"Yes, I know." She patted her tummy and added, "And look where it got me."

"Are you happy about the baby, Amelia?"

"Absolutely."

"You don't mind too much that it's my child?"

"How could I regret anything about this baby?"

"Is it a girl or a boy?"

"I don't know."

"You didn't have the test?"

"No. How do you know about ultrasounds?"

He shrugged. The gesture reminded her he was damn near naked.

Anxious to change the subject before he launched into a discussion of how they were going to raise a child Ryder would not even want to acknowledge after his memory came back, she said, "Did the jump into the pool help?"

"No."

"Nothing?"

He looked from the sparkling water to the tree branches laced together above their heads. "It's like a place I've visited in a dream. One second, it's all as real as you and me standing here, and the next, it's gone, like a song you can't pin down. I have the tune sometimes, but never long enough, and the lyrics always drift away."

"It'll get better," she said. Then nodding briefly, she left him to dress in private, her thoughts an uneasy companion as she started the long climb back up the hill.

Chapter Six

Ryder wasn't going to admit it to Amelia, but the morning had taken a toll. He swallowed a couple of coated aspirin when she wasn't looking. She didn't seem to want to chat on the way to his college, which was okay with him. His head felt as if an angry judge was running loose in there with a giant gavel.

He noticed the metaphor he'd chosen at once and it made him think of the Victorian house that was his office. He needed to go into work for an hour or two. He could sit at his desk, if he still had one, and try to remember exactly what it was he used to do. Maybe the sight of his colleagues would work the magic that would unlock his memory. It couldn't hurt.

Besides, it would give him and Amelia some time apart. He had no earthly idea why he'd ever wanted to resist her before. All he knew was that staying away from her was now becoming increasingly difficult.

She was addictive. She was soft and she smelled great. Her hair was fascinating, a hundred shades of gold, from the color of the yellow weeds in the field they'd climbed, to the tawny mane of a lion. He loved her arms, long and slender. He was dying to see her shoulders bare. She had a beautiful throat and a chin that absolutely begged to be kissed. And her lips...well, her lips.

But it was more. He'd told her the truth that morning when he'd said she was warm and compassionate and funny. He loved the way her eyes flashed when she was angry, and how she constantly seemed to second-guess that anger, as though her inherent humanity made getting mad at him difficult for her. She was troubled by her feelings, he could see that. Being with him was difficult for her.

She was a decent, good person, he thought.

He must have pushed her into an intolerable corner for her to have grown so distrustful of him.

Well, of course he had. She'd told him all about it. And yet she stayed.

He wanted to wipe the past from her memory. He wanted her to see him for who he was now. But she was so grounded in yesterday that she constantly erected road-blocks, and when he occasionally got through one of those, she seemed to build even higher ones.

Still, he found his fingers itching to touch her again. She'd said they shouldn't kiss—that was preposterous. They were born to be together—he could sense it. Couldn't she? He slid her a sideways glance. She was staring straight ahead and was obviously having no trouble controlling her feelings for him.

"This is it," Amelia said as she slowed the car.

He discovered the campus was situated on several tree-lined blocks. The buildings were huge, square, brick af-fairs with small windows. A few newer structures peeked through here and there, standing out like concrete sore thumbs.

"Let's park and walk," he said.

They found a spot to park without too much trouble even though summer classes were obviously in session. Amelia pointed at a building across the street. "That was your fraternity," she said.

He looked at the sign above the door, and the symbol looked familiar. It was on the tip of his tongue to blurt out this news when he realized it looked familiar because of his fraternity ring. With a glance at his hand, he turned away from the shuttered building.

"Nothing?" she said.

"No." He closed his eyes and rubbed the back of his neck as he took a few steps. For a second, he thought about the river and the temporary bliss he'd felt. The cool water, the sight of Amelia, all legs and blond hair, her mysterious gray eyes, her lips struggling with a grin. The vague feeling of belonging he'd felt had joined forces with the relief to be out of the blasted hospital, to be alive and feeling good, to be with the mother of his child.

To be with Amelia.

Again, he had the piercing worry that she would try to raise the baby without him. He glanced at her. She was staring at the sidewalk, as deep in her thoughts as he was in his.

"What are your plans?" he asked.

That earned him a quick look. "My plans?"

"I'm a little slow on the uptake here, Amelia, but it has just occurred to me that I don't know a thing about you. Like where you live, for instance."

"I...I don't have a place right now," she said.

"Why not?"

"Because I moved out of it before your accident. I

stayed with your parents while you were in the hospital and now, as you know, I'm staying with you.''

''Where you belong,'' he said firmly.

''No.''

''But the baby—''

''No,'' she repeated, casting him a chilly, gray gaze that was like a fog bank creeping over the bay.

''This is my child, too,'' he said evenly as he rubbed his temples.

''Yes, I know.''

''So if you won't live with me, where are you going to go? You're going to get a place close by, I assume?''

''Your head hurts. I brought your pain pills—''

''Stop avoiding my question.''

''I don't know what I'm going to do,'' she finally said.

''Then stay with me,'' he said quietly.

Amelia resumed walking. Exasperated, he joined her. His solution to her housing problem seemed logical to him. Why was she fighting it? And why had she given up her apartment? Instinct told him he'd better lay off for the time being. He said, ''I really appreciate the fact that you're helping me.''

She nodded without meeting his gaze.

''I couldn't handle all this without you.''

''You'd be fine.''

''No,'' he insisted.

She stopped again and faced him. ''You have your family, Ryder. When your parents get back, you'll get to know them again. They're wonderful people. They'll help you.''

It sounded as though she was telling him good-bye two weeks in advance. He said, ''I don't know my family. They're strangers.'' Was there panic in his voice? Or was it his throbbing head distorting things?

"You'll get to know them again, trust me."

"How about your family?"

"All I have left is an aunt and her husband in Nevada. They own a little furniture store."

"Are you going to teach after the baby is born?"

She looked up at him again. "My plans to teach are on hold for now. I have just enough money to be independent for a couple of years if I'm careful. I've gained fifteen and a half pounds so far, at least as of three weeks ago. I am careful not to eat the wrong foods or drink alcohol or smoke, not that I ever have anyway. I indulge myself daily with one cup of coffee. Is there anything else you want to know?"

He ignored her barb, knowing that the old Ryder most likely deserved it. "When is your next doctor's appointment?"

"I made one for a little over a week from now."

"May I go with you?"

She hesitated.

"Please?" he added.

"It's...complicated," she finally said.

"Why?"

"Let me think about it."

"What's to think about?"

She shook her head and looked so uncomfortable that he decided to cut her some slack. "I just want you to know that I plan on helping out—financially, being only one way."

"I don't mean to be unkind, Ryder, but I can take care of myself."

"But the baby—"

"Is fine. I will make sure the baby is fine. I told you that before we broke up months ago. It doesn't really matter how you're feeling right this minute. The truth of the matter remains the same—you didn't want a baby then, and when you regain your memory, you'll realize you don't really want one now."

"Amelia—"

"And if you persist in talking to me about this, I'm going to leave."

Did she mean leave him at the campus to find his own way home, leave his house, or leave as in never coming back? He didn't want to find out. He said, "Are you hungry?"

"Yes."

"There's the cafeteria. How about some gray vegetables and green meat?"

She looked up abruptly. "Do you remember the food being awful here?"

"Isn't it?"

"It was when I went here, but how did you know?"

"The smell wafting over the campus."

"Maybe eating here will jog loose a memory," she said.

"Maybe it'll be the kind of memory I could live without," he added.

Amelia ordered a fruit salad, thinking there wasn't much anyone could do to ruin it. Ryder tried to eat a chicken sandwich, but he kept rubbing his forehead and the back of his neck.

She should have figured out a way to keep him from exerting himself that morning. She could only imagine what his doctors would say if they'd been witness to his shenanigans.

As she stabbed at a strawberry, she heard her name and looked up in time to see an old friend approaching. Steve Johnson stopped by the side of her table and, ignoring Ryder, took her hand. "Amelia," he said fondly, then leaned down and kissed the top of her head.

She hadn't seen Steve for months, since they'd shared an early childhood development class and a few dates after she broke up with Ryder and before she discovered she was pregnant. She patted the bench next to her and he sat down, his eyes glued to her face.

"It is astoundingly good to see you," Steve said. "I heard about the baby."

"It's great to see you, too."

"I tried calling, but your phone was disconnected."

"I...moved," she said vaguely.

Ryder cleared his throat and Amelia made late introductions, hoping Steve wouldn't mention her plans to move to Nevada. He'd been her confidant after the breakup. Amelia now regretted saying anything, though if memory served her right, she hadn't really said much. Apparently, however, she'd said enough because he was decidedly cool toward Ryder.

It was a relief when Steve finally made apologies about an appointment he had to keep. He stood, his eyes kind, and said, "Amelia, remember I'll always be here for you and the baby."

"Thanks, Steve."

Ryder said firmly, "She has me."

Steve frowned. "We'll see."

Standing, Ryder announced, "I admit I've made some terrible mistakes, but I *will* be here for her. For both of them."

"I guess there's a first time for everything," Steve mumbled.

Amelia said, "Please..."

Steve regarded Ryder for a brief moment, then relented, saying nothing further. He smiled at her. "Okay, angel." Leaning down, cupping her chin briefly in his left hand, he kissed her cheek and then he was gone.

"Angel?" Ryder said. "Who was that?"

"I told you who it was."

"Amelia—"

"Don't start with me. I have friends, too. That's the end of it, right there."

"Okay, I'll accept that. But you need to accept what I said as the truth."

He frowned down at his food, and Amelia was ready to abandon her meal. Eating in the cafeteria had been a bad idea all around.

She was folding her napkin when a woman of about sixty, carrying a tray that held the same fruit salad that had just lost its appeal for Amelia, paused by their table.

"Rob Hogan?" the woman said hopefully.

Amelia inwardly groaned, wishing too late that they had found a nice remote restaurant in which to dine. First Steve, and now this woman whose greeting left Ryder looking as though someone had knifed him. He put down his sandwich and said, "No. I'm sorry—"

"Then you're Ryder," she said with a subtle change to her voice. "Imagine seeing you back on this campus."

He pushed his lunch aside.

"I'd heard you were still practicing law in Seaport. How's Rob?"

Ryder looked at Amelia who couldn't help him. "I'm sorry," he said. "I've been in an accident. Do I know you?"

Her lined face was concerned. "Oh, my."

"It happened this summer," he added.

"I was away until August first. I'm Kendra Platt. I teach here. History. I had both of you in classes."

"Oh."

"And how is Rob? I don't have to tell you how much I admire that brother of yours. I know he's in California now, more the pity because I never see him."

"Actually—"

The woman continued, ignoring Ryder's attempt to interrupt. "I get Christmas cards from him every year, though. Such a sweet man. I always knew he would be the kind of lawyer who looked out for the little guy." She patted the top of Ryder's shoulder and added, "Not that defending criminals isn't honorable, too. In this country, we are all innocent until proven guilty. Of course, so many criminal lawyers don't even want to know the truth because it might hinder their ability to get some monster off with a light sentence." She paused and added, "Not that you ever would."

"Ms. Platt—"

"It's just that Rob had something extra going for him. I imagine he'll do wonderful things with his life."

Ryder raised his voice. "Ms. Platt!"

She blinked a few times. "What is it?"

"Rob died in the accident that left me without a memory."

She appeared stunned. "Robert...died?"

"Yes," Ryder said. "I'm sorry."

The woman mumbled her apologies and, tears brimming in her eyes, hurried off to a far corner of the cafeteria.

Ryder looked at Amelia. The pain in his head showed in his eyes and her heart went out to him. She opened her purse and took out the small brown container. Setting it in front of him, she said, "Maybe it's time to give up and take a pain pill."

Wordlessly, he took one of the pills and downed it with a gulp of ice water.

"I think we'd better go now."

"Yes," he said.

They walked back to the car. Amelia was growing increasingly concerned about him. It was hard to believe that this was the same man who had dropped from a rope into a pool of water a mere three hours before. The same man who had carried her down a slope and kissed her in a way that sent every fiber of her body into overload. That man had been strong and sure of himself, full of life, on top of his world, no matter how fuzzy it was. This man looked defeated and exhausted.

Was Ryder well enough to pick up on the unfavorable vibes emanating from Kendra Platt? Wouldn't he have to be in a coma not to?

Back in the car, he fell asleep almost at once, giving Amelia plenty of time to worry. She thought about driving him to the hospital, but decided against it. Maybe all he needed was a few hours' rest and a little less excitement.

She should be in Nevada by now, buying wallpaper for the nursery. Aunt Jenny and her husband, Lou, had lived in the house since Amelia's dad had died. The plan had been that Amelia would finish her education, take a job on the Oregon coast, and after a few years, return to Nevada and her roomy old childhood house. Toward that end, she'd saved the modest inheritance her father had left her.

That plan had gone out the window when Amelia learned she was pregnant. Happily, Jenny and Lou, who were only a few years her senior, had asked if they might stay on. Lou said the baby would need a strong male influence and he was just the guy for the job. Jenny had hinted that they were contemplating starting a family of their own and some hands-on practice would be just the ticket.

Thanks to them, the decision to leave Seaport and Ryder and Ryder's family had been manageable. The money in the bank would allow her two years, maybe three, if she was careful, to stay home and care for her child. Sure, she'd made some major mistakes in the recent past, but she was fully capable of fixing them.

That was where she should be right now. She should be thinking about yellow ducks and green turtles. She should be learning to knit. She should be helping Lou refinish her grandmother's rocker and planting flowers in the warm, sandy earth. She should be catching glimpses of her ever-burgeoning silhouette in the large beveled mirror mounted beside the front door. She should be home...making a nest, getting ready. Home.

Ryder awoke as they entered the outskirts of Seaport. He felt groggy and thirsty, but at least the unrelenting headache was gone. He sat up straight and stared at Amelia who cast him a worried frown.

"How are you feeling?"

"Much better," he said. "I guess I overdid it today."

"No kidding."

"I promised I wouldn't whine about it."

"You haven't whined. Your macho male image is still intact."

"Is a macho male image important to me?"

"Frankly, Ryder, I believe a macho male image is important to most men."

"Even Steve?"

She turned to look at him. "Even Steve."

He gazed out the window as the newly familiar scent of the sea became stronger. This was his hometown.

Surely, buried somewhere inside him, was recognition of the trees and the gulls and the crescent bay. Somewhere inside him, he must feel protected by just being here. How did he get to that deep inner spot?

Certainly not by talking to his old teachers, that was for sure. He felt bad that Ms. Platt had to find out about Rob's death in such a blunt way, but her words had been thoughtless, bordering on cruel. Once again, he found himself saddened by the fact that he must have spent so much of his life being a jerk that people felt compelled to talk to him the way she had.

Like Steve. Ryder could tell Amelia had confided in Steve and it made his blood boil. Yet how could he blame her for looking to another man for comfort after the heel he'd been? The question now playing Ping-Pong in his sorry excuse for a brain was this—how much comfort had Steve given?

Just then, he spotted a low-level building hugging the cliff above the bay. The sign in the parking lot was covered with red, yellow and orange neon peppers.

"Pull in over there," he said.

Amelia did as he asked. "What is it?"

"Probably nothing, but there's a napkin in the book by my reading chair at the house. It's from here."

She looked at the sign. "Pepper's Place?"

"Did we ever come here together?"

"No."

"Why?"

"You didn't invite me."

"Why not? Do you know?"

She studied him in a way he was beginning to recognize. It meant she had something relatively unpleasant to say and was trying to figure out how to sugarcoat it. He said, "Just tell me, Amelia."

She shrugged, looked away from him. "From what I hear, this is one of the places you come to pick up women."

He stared at the innocuous structure. It was only four in the afternoon, so there weren't many cars in the parking lot yet. He said, "I guess we'd better go inside."

"Not me."

"Why not?"

"There's probably enough secondhand smoke in there to choke an elephant. I'll wait out here."

"Will you be okay?"

"Just go."

Because of a wide overhang, a row of windows facing the bay didn't lift the dark atmosphere of the building he entered. Posters of hot sauces decorated the walls. A long bar ran along the back. Strings of peppers, both the real kind and ceramic make-believes, hung from rafters. There was a wooden dance floor breaking the red carpet. One small table held two people holding hands over beer mugs. The other tables were empty.

He took a seat at the bar. The only other customers were a woman at the end who was in the process of lighting a cigarette, and two men staring at a televised ball game without any sound. For a place that looked as though it tended to be lively, it was quiet and kind of morose.

The bartender turned around from where he'd been washing out glasses. His face broke into a big smile.

"Ryder!" he said, sticking out a hand as he advanced. "It's good to see you, man."

Ryder shook the bartender's hand.

The man was about thirty, tall with a bushy black mustache. Ryder said, "It's good to see you...."

The bartender raised his eyebrows. "Nick. Nick

Swope. Don't you remember me? You are Ryder Hogan, aren't you?"

Ryder shook his hand. "Nice to see you again, Nick. I've been in an accident and my memory is a little...spotty."

"That's too bad, man. You want the usual?"

"A margarita?"

"Stirred, not blended, I know, I know. Hey, there's a friend of yours down there. Lily has been asking about you." A couple of quick jerks of Nick's head indicated Lily was the woman at the end of the bar.

"I don't remember her and I can't drink right now, Nick, so how about iced tea?"

"I guess there's a first time for everything."

"How often did I come around here?" he asked as Nick set a tall, icy glass down on a coaster in front of him. He was vaguely aware Lily had left her seat.

"Every Saturday night, like clockwork."

"I must have had some good times here."

"The best," Nick said with a wink. There was a wall of photos behind the bar and Nick pointed to one. Ryder saw himself sandwiched between two beautiful women. It looked as though he was enjoying himself.

"I was hoping being here might help me remember things," Ryder said.

He felt a hand on his arm. "Maybe I can help with that. I know all about what happened to you," Lily said as she inhaled on her cigarette. "Claude told me. He works out in Bridgeville now, running the emergency truck out of the firehouse." She exhaled smoke slowly, slightly upward, and added, "He's the one who pulled you and your brother out of the wrecked car. He said you have amnesia."

"He seems well informed," Ryder said.

"Oh, sure, Claude knows Jerry Hill. He's the cop assigned to your case. Jerry even asked me questions about you. Claude said he never saw so much blood at the accident. He said your brother's face was cut up real bad—"

"Please, no more," Ryder interrupted, holding up one hand.

She shrugged and Ryder took a closer look at her. She had chin-length black hair, heavy eye makeup, thin lips plumped out with red lipstick. She was attractive but not pretty, not wholesome, not captivating...not Amelia. Judging from the way she clung to his arm, it seemed they were more than just friends. He wondered how he could politely ask her to stop blowing smoke in his face and let go of his arm.

Grinding out her half-finished cigarette in an ashtray, regarding him from beneath lowered lashes, she said, "Why don't we go to your place? You having amnesia, it would be like the first time."

"I'm living with someone now," he said, hoping Amelia never found out he'd worded it that way.

"So?"

"So, she might not like it."

"Then we can go to my place."

"Truth of the matter is, the woman I'm living with is expecting a baby. I don't want to run around on her."

Lily regarded him with narrowed eyes. "You've changed."

"I hope so. I'm trying."

"Don't try too hard," she said with a quick smile. "There was nothing wrong with the way you were. So, who is the lucky little woman?"

"Her name is Amelia," he said, immediately wondering if he should have mentioned a name. It was too late to snap it back…he'd just leave off her last name.

"The little schoolteacher you told me about? So, she finally trapped you, huh?"

"Trapped me?"

"Yeah. I told you to be careful. That kind always thinks having a kid is the way to get a guy."

"Who trapped him?" Nick asked as he refilled the empty iced tea glass.

"That schoolteacher friend of his went and got herself knocked up."

"Hey, man, listen, a word of advice from a guy who knows. I had a buddy who had some girl do the same thing and then he found out the kid wasn't even his."

Ryder looked from one helpful face to the other. His headache had started again with the mention of Detective Hill's name, and now, with this talk about Amelia, it was throbbing. He pulled two dollars—all the cash he had— out of his wallet and put it on the bar.

"Don't look so down, lover," Lily crooned as he left.

Nick called out, "See you next Saturday night?"

Ryder couldn't wait to get out of Pepper's Place.

"How was it?" Amelia asked as she fanned the air between them when he rejoined her in the car. The smoke must have permeated his clothing. When he didn't answer immediately, she narrowed her eyes and added, "Are you okay?"

For a moment, he just stared at her. After learning how he'd betrayed Amelia by talking about her to other people, he was more certain than ever that he didn't deserve her concern, and yet here she was, offering it. How big was her heart? Big enough to forgive him?

He put a hand against her cheek, marveling at the petal softness of her skin. She blinked rapidly, as though his touch affected her, and it sparked in him a glimmer of hope that they could find their way back to each other.

"What happened in there?"

"More of the same thing that's been happening ever since this nightmare began," he said huskily, suddenly overcome with emotion. "Amelia, I have to ask you, I need to know. Can you forgive me? Will you forgive me?"

She looked perplexed. "Forgive you for what?"

He took both her hands in his and held on tight. "For taking you for granted," he said at last.

A bittersweet smile played across her lips. "I suppose we're all guilty of occasionally taking each other for granted, Ryder."

"What I'm trying to say, Amelia, is that I'm sorry."

She bit her luscious lower lip. He took a chance and opened his arms, willing her to accept his embrace, longing for the chance to hold her.

Scooting across the seat, she came to him, willingly, with the trust he didn't deserve, the trust he yearned for more than anything else in the world.

"Thank you," he whispered against her ear.

Later that night, sitting beside Ryder on the white brocade sofa, Amelia opened the first of the four albums Nina had left. She sat silently as Ryder looked at photographs that traced his family from wedding pictures of his parents through baby pictures of two roly-poly dark-haired baby boys.

In one photo after the other, the twins' lives were chronicled along with their older brother, Philip. Amelia saw pictures of them in their mother's arms, riding tandem piggy-back on their father. She saw them taking their first steps and sitting in matching highchairs. And she was struck, as she had been the one and only time she saw the two brothers together, how alike they looked.

If she had a son, was this how he would look? She gazed intently at the small faces in the album, at the dark, mischievous eyes and plump cheeks, at the smiles.

Patting her tummy, she decided she wouldn't mind if her baby looked just like his father. At one time, the thought that this might be the case had distressed her. But spending time with Ryder now, she found herself reaping a side benefit. The Ryder who had lied to her and used her was also the man who sat beside her, quietly trying to find his past. They were part and parcel of the same man, and she couldn't help it, she liked him.

Why hadn't he shown her more of this side when they were dating? Why had he felt the need to hide himself from her? She'd thought they were intimate and now she realized they had never really achieved the kind of intimacy they were beginning to forge right here, right now. Oh, brother. This pool of confusion in which she dog-paddled had a decided undercurrent.

The next album moved through their childhood—standing in front of the bus on their first day of school, identical gap-toothed grins; holding kittens and puppies; posing with soccer balls and baseball bats; riding bikes.

After grammar school, pictures of the twins together grew fewer and farther between. Ryder looked carefully at labeled pictures of himself playing baseball, and labeled pictures of Rob doing the same. But they played for different teams, evidenced by the colors of their jerseys. And then there were snapshots of them in high school, with different girls all wearing fancy corsages and youthful smiles of great expectations.

That left only two more albums to go, but as Amelia hefted the second to last onto her lap, Ryder put his hand over hers to prevent her from opening the cover. "Let's save it for tomorrow night," he said wearily. Brushing his hair aside, he added, "I'm afraid they didn't help."

"Maybe the doctor was right. Maybe it's just going to take time," Amelia said as she put aside the album.

He leaned his head against the sofa back, folding his hands together over his chest, his long legs crossed at the ankles in front of him. He'd been quiet all evening, as though ruminating on something he didn't want to share. His cheeks looked hollow and she tried to remember if he'd eaten anything besides a piece of fruit that day. Lunch had been a disaster and dinner was a blur.

Again, she was struck with the sweet torment of being so close to him their thighs touched. He always felt a few degrees warmer than she and the warmth seemed to pulse outward from his body, infiltrating the air around her skin, making her impossibly aware of him.

He said, "You're going to have a very beautiful baby, Amelia Enderling." Slowly, he put his hand on her maternity shirt. "Have you felt the baby move yet?"

"Yes," she whispered. "For quite awhile now."

"Do you think I could?"

"The baby must be asleep," Amelia choked out.

"Maybe we can wake the little guy up," Ryder said, and leaning over her, he stared into her eyes.

This time, when his lips met hers, she refused to think—period. This time, she opened her mouth and felt his tongue touch hers, and the world took on an added dimension of sensation, warm and wonderful. She felt his hand move beneath her shirt. She heard herself moan as she closed her eyes. He touched her breasts through her bra and she felt an overwhelming desire to lie naked, exposed, with him.

Her head was whirling. She felt hot, dizzy, faint. She

wanted him to kiss her until the end of the world swallowed them both and there was no tomorrow to remind her of the foolishness of this moment.

Slowly, slowly, she came back to her senses. Kissing Ryder was like being caught in a rip tide, but she gently pushed on his chest, fighting the feel of the firm flesh beneath his shirt, struggling to regain her balance and composure.

"I know I loved you once," he said, his voice husky, his lips touching her brow as he formed the words. He kissed her cheek, her lips again, her throat.

And I loved you, she thought, but she wouldn't say it, not now, not ever again. An incredible sadness settled over her heart.

"Don't fight it," he whispered against her ear.

Amelia decided what was desperately needed was a dose of reality, for her as well as for him. Disengaging herself from his embrace, she mumbled, "I...I told you before, Ryder. You weren't ever really in love with me."

"I don't believe you," he said.

"It's the truth. Learning I was pregnant did nothing but upset you."

He leaned back, as though trying to focus on her face in order to gauge her reaction as he blurted out, "Is that why Rob and I were driving around together that night?"

"I don't know," she said, hedging. This question was dangerously close to revealing that Ryder was the driver of the doomed vehicle. She stood abruptly and stacked the albums, her hands shaky, her knees wobbly.

He sat up straight and drilled her with his gaze. "Doesn't it seem odd to you that we left Philip's wedding and went off like that? And why is Detective Hill asking people questions about me?"

Amelia froze at the mention of Hill's name. She'd been

under the impression the police were going to give Ryder a few weeks to recover his memory. She said, "Detective Hill? How do you know he's been asking around about you?"

"Someone at Pepper's Place mentioned it," he mumbled.

"I'm sure if he's asking questions, it's just routine."

Ryder got to his feet. As he stepped in front of her and she was forced to crane her neck back to meet his gaze, her breath caught in her throat. There was something in his eyes, something personal. "Amelia, did you use your pregnancy to...to trap me?"

She mumbled, "No, of course not. Where did you get such an idea?"

He shifted his weight slightly. "It doesn't matter."

The thought came like a thunderbolt. "Does this mean you've remembered talking to me at Philip's wedding?"

He looked crestfallen. "You told me you were pregnant at my brother's wedding?"

"Yes."

"And I accused you of trying to trap me?"

"Yes," she said uneasily. On the defensive now, she barked, "Who told you about this?"

"Someone at Pepper's."

"You said that."

"A woman," he elaborated.

"I see."

That meant that before he'd even known about the pregnancy, he'd confided in another woman that the silly schoolteacher was trying to trap him.

Amelia recalled the way Ryder had looked after coming out of Pepper's Place. In retrospect, she realized that he'd been ashamed of his past behavior. That was why he'd asked her to forgive him for taking her for granted.

And like a woman in love, she'd readily agreed. How could he go from that caring, sensitive man to this distrustful one is such a short time?

Fists clenched, she added, "Do you believe it?"

"I don't know what to believe," he said, turning away.

She started to grasp his sleeve, but she let her hand drop.

It's the old Ryder surfacing, with the old fears and the old suspicions.

A few moments of uncomfortable silence was broken when he turned and said, "I'm going to make myself an omelette. Want one?"

Quicksilver. That, too, was an old trait, moving from one thought or idea or emotion to the next without bringing anything to a satisfactory conclusion.

She nodded, but what she really wanted was the tenderness of the afternoon, the trust she'd felt budding between them. It was suddenly clear to her that she wasn't doing a very good job of protecting her heart. With her baby's future at stake, she vowed to be more careful.

Chapter Seven

Night after night, Ryder had the same dream—he was alone, running. Then it was dark, and he was driving a car. Oh, the freedom! Gradually, he became aware he had a passenger and he turned to see who it was. All he found was a mirror, strapped into the seat like a human being. He looked...if only he could see...

That was when he always woke up, breathing hard, chest heaving, panic at full force for no reason he could fathom. He would try to rationalize the fear away, but eventually it would drift off on its own.

Like it did this morning...

The sound of running water was something he could grasp. Gradually, it occurred to him that it came from the guest bath so Amelia must be taking her morning shower. He immediately thought of her rounded breasts and hips, the ever-increasing bulge of his baby.

It was *his* baby, wasn't it?

For days, the bartender's warning had echoed in his head. He tried not to dwell on it—heaven knew he already had enough crazy thoughts to keep him busy—but he kept seeing Amelia's friend, Steve. The way he had looked at Amelia, the way he had kissed her. The memory was driving him nuts.

Ryder realized he'd taken Amelia's claim she was carrying his child at face value.

But why would she lie about it when she consistently made it very clear she wasn't interested in him? Was he such a prize?

Not in his current condition. And judging from what he'd learned about his past, not then either. Unless he was heir to a fortune he knew nothing about, Amelia Enderling had no reason to lie about the baby's paternity.

Besides, did it matter? Was his growing infatuation with Amelia linked only to her pregnancy with his child?

No.

Crazy thoughts. Almost as scary as thinking about Detective Hill asking questions, or the accident he couldn't remember.

Sitting on the side of the bed, he ran a hand through his hair. For a week, he had done little but hang out around the house, listening to music, reading. Amelia, on the other hand, was a whirlwind, packing his books, one by one, into the living room, arranging them close to his reading chair where she announced they belonged. She fixed him delicious meals he had little appetite for, and then, in the evening, settled on the sofa to do some kind of handwork on a very tiny garment. Embroidery, that was what it was. She was embroidering little yellow ducks around the neck of a sweet little white thing, her lips curved into the most serene smile as she worked.

Occasionally they went to the hospital to see one of his doctors or shopped for food, but what he liked the best were the hours they spent talking, Amelia valiantly trying to remember every detail of every day they had spent together.

She had loved him, he could tell. And if she had loved him once, she could love him again.

Still, it was obviously an unpleasant chore for her. He was always on the verge of telling her she could quit, but never did. He wasn't willing to surrender the way her voice filled his head and kept his brain from rattling around alone in there. And so, selfishly, he kept her talking.

Philip had visited twice, the first time alone, the second time with his new bride, Sara. Neither visit had sparked any memories in Ryder and he'd been relieved when they were over.

The best times came late every afternoon when Amelia dragged a mat out from behind the sofa and did her exercises. Looking over the top of a book, watching her twist and contort, he was both fascinated and frustrated. Dressed in black leotards and a loose gray-blue shirt that brought out the subtle color of her eyes, she did leg lifts that set his heart thumping, or sat crossed-legged, back as straight as an arrow, reaching for the stars with elegant arms, revolving her neck, exposing such tender skin that his mouth almost watered.

It seemed unlikely he had ever before found the sight of a pregnant woman so erotic.

So the question was, did he stand a chance to win her back?

According to her, he didn't really want her back. According to the people who knew him, he didn't want anyone. But that was not what he felt in his heart.

When they had kissed a few nights before, she'd responded. Or was the response something he conjured in his sleep to comfort himself?

He reviewed what he knew.

Amelia and he had met at his office. She must have seemed so different from the usual women he dated—less worldly, less experienced, honest and straightforward...pure. Knowing what he knew of his own personality as gathered from the last few weeks, she'd no doubt presented a major challenge.

So, he'd seduced her. And when she was no longer everything he coveted, he'd dumped her.

Except, having sex with him hadn't changed who and what she was. Hadn't he known that?

Apparently not. He'd moved on to Lily or some other woman. Months went by during which he apparently forgot all about Amelia until she showed up at Philip's wedding.

What had that been like, to look around and see her? Had his heart raced? Had he been pleased?

Probably not. Curious, yes. Pleased, no. He would have wondered what she wanted after all this time.

That was when she'd told him she was having his baby, and according to her, he'd been angry. Furious! He'd told her she was trying to use a baby to trap him. That had obviously been a concern—her wanting more from a relationship than he did—long before the baby was conceived, maybe even before they broke up. How else would Lily know about it?

A flash of light pierced his brain and was gone, but for half a millisecond the memory of that day shimmered behind his weary eyeballs. He could almost remember the rage storming around and inside him like an invasive holocaust.

It was there—and then it wasn't.

He shook his head again and started where he'd left off. Angry. Maybe Rob had tried to talk to him. Maybe they had left so they could go somewhere quiet. Out on an old road? So far out of town they weren't found for hours?

A new thought struck him. Had Rob died right away, or had he lived awhile? And if he had lived, had he been conscious, and if so, had he been able to speak? If they had talked, had they settled things?

Was it possible that because of Rob, Ryder had experienced a moment of epiphany before he lost consciousness and Rob died? Could that explain the new way he saw things, the new way he felt about becoming a father, his new attitude toward Amelia and about life in general? Had coming close to death touched him, changed him, improved him?

Could that have happened?

The sound of running water stopped. He got to his feet and stared at the wall as though he had laser vision, as though he could see through the paint and the drywall and the wallpaper and tile, as though he could see Amelia standing there. At last, he dropped his eyes and went to take his own shower.

Amelia struggled to hide the fact that she was going stir-crazy. She knew that this quiet week had been good for Ryder's recovery, but it had been difficult for her.

All this enforced closeness was taking a toll.

A dozen times she'd come close to packing her bag. A dozen times she'd decided looking out for herself was looking out for her baby and hence wasn't really selfish but wise. And a dozen times she'd imagined the look in Ryder's eyes when he realized she was gone. It always stopped her.

"Are you sure I like grapefruit?" he grumbled as she

sat across the table from him nursing her beloved cup of coffee.

She glanced up. After days of rest, she thought it odd that he looked more tired this morning than ever. She also noticed for the first time that over the last few weeks, his thick hair had grown until it was now long on his neck and flopped beguilingly onto his forehead. He was obviously overdue for a haircut, something he would never have allowed in his old state.

His face kept getting more and more angular, probably because he didn't seem to have an appetite. She had heard him fighting his sheets during the night. She had lain awake, wondering if his dreams were dependent on his shallow memory pool and if so, what new demons caused him such distress.

This morning, his lingering looks at her appeared haunted. And his haunted look gave him a sensual appeal she had to firmly counsel herself to ignore.

She said, "Yes, you like grapefruit."

"Well, I don't like it anymore," he said as he pushed the bowl away.

Mentioning the subject she broached every morning, she added, "You know, your folks will be home soon. Maybe today we can finish with those picture albums."

"Today is your doctor's appointment."

"Not until this afternoon," she said, wondering how she was going to get out of taking Ryder with her. Apparently, she wasn't. He seemed adamant, and part of her wanted him there, just once. Trouble was, he needed to be prepared for the "situation" she had created at the clinic, but try as she might, she couldn't think of a way to come clean that didn't make her sound desperate and foolish and just plain stupid.

Maybe everyone there, especially the chatty receptionist, would be too busy to say anything awkward.

Amelia crossed her fingers.

"You aren't backing out of your decision to let me tag along, are you?"

She looked up abruptly. "I wasn't aware I had actually agreed."

"Maybe not in so many words."

"It'll be boring—"

"No."

"Then—"

"No excuses. It's important to me. Baby appointment today, the office of Goodman, Todd and Flanders next week. If I can't remember my past, I'll build a here and now."

He sounded doggedly determined. But then, Ryder was always determined. "Well, anyway, about the picture albums—"

"I don't think so."

That was what he always said and she never pushed. This time she said, "Why not? They're the more recent ones—"

"They're full of pictures of strangers."

"But it's you and your family—"

"Exactly." He thumped both elbows on the table, laced his fingers, and rested his chin on his hands. His stare was intense and traveled through Amelia, pinning her to the dining room chair. Finally he said, "There's something I've been wanting to talk to you about."

She inwardly groaned. Before she could divert him, he added, "When I kissed you the other night, you kissed me back."

She'd expected a discussion on the upcoming doctor

appointment or her plans for the future, not kissing. She mumbled, "No, I didn't."

"Don't lie to me, Amelia."

"Ryder—"

"Things are confusing enough without lies."

Biting her lip, she returned his stare. Fair was fair. She said, "Okay, I won't lie to you. Yes, I kissed you back."

"Why?"

Amelia put down her mug. Did he have to ask? Didn't he ever see himself reflected in her eyes the way she sometimes saw herself in his? Didn't he catch her staring at him, lingering near him when they occasionally stood close to each other doing the dishes or folding clothes? Didn't he have any idea how her breath shortened when he touched her?

And didn't he realize how desperately she was trying to ignore these feelings?

She said, "You've always had a way of getting to me. Physically, I mean."

His stare penetrated her. "Then that's all it was between us, physical?"

"Yes."

"You have no...feelings for me?"

"Of course I have feelings for you."

"But you don't love me?"

"Of course not." She said it automatically because she had to, feeling guilty because she knew it was a lie and she'd just promised not to lie. But what good would be served by telling him that she'd fallen for him again? Who would it help?

She'd loved Ryder once upon a time, enough to agree to marry him, enough to make love with him. He'd been fun and attentive and she'd been infatuated. He'd broken her heart, she'd finally seen him for what he was, she'd let him go. Physical attraction aside, she'd understood that he was a man destined to skim over life, attracting people as he went, never forming a bond that stood a chance of enduring through the trials of married life.

And then the accident.

This new Ryder was still fun, still attentive, attractive as all get out, and incredibly sexy. But he was more complex than before. More thoughtful. A man who seemed to embrace life on a level commensurate with his intelligence.

Ryder was turning into the man Amelia had once thought him to be. And she was getting in deeper and deeper.

He said, "What if I were to tell you that I feel something more for you, Amelia?"

She closed her eyes. Was he saying he loved her? How many times had she dreamed of this moment and then chided herself for courting fairy tales? She opened her eyes again and found him staring at her.

He wasn't the man he once was, at least not at this second in time. This man was trying to tell her about his feelings which were obviously making him as miserable as they were making her. He had tricked and deceived her before, and yet she couldn't help but believe that what Ryder was saying and feeling now was real.

And impossible.

She said, "For all intents and purposes you've only known me a few weeks. I'm the one person you see and talk to on a regular basis. Your feelings aren't reliable right now, can't you see that?"

Ryder had always had a way of brushing aside details he didn't want to address. Now he said, "Did you know Rob?"

She felt a prickling sensation behind her nose as she said, "I only met him once."

"What was he like?"

"We only talked for a few minutes. He was warm and charming and exceedingly kind."

"And I'm the resident monster," Ryder said bitterly.

Placing her own anger about Ryder's guilt for Rob's death in a secret spot in her heart, she said, "You're not a monster, Ryder. Especially not anymore."

"But you keep waiting for me to metamorphose back into the womanizing beast of yesterday."

"I know I do. That's why it might be better if someone else—"

"No," he said emphatically.

"Then maybe the next album—"

He held up a hand and with a smile that was devastating simply because it came so naturally, he said, "Please, no more pictures."

"Well, Philip called while you were in the shower and invited us to his house. How about that?"

He shrugged. "I don't know Philip."

"He's your brother," she said softly.

"I know."

"Then maybe we could—"

"Where did I grow up?"

"A couple of miles from here."

"Is the house still there?"

"Yes."

"Do we have time before your appointment to go see it?"

"Sure," she said, torn with unease over the thought of the pending appointment and joy at escaping an apartment that grew smaller with each passing minute.

This time he insisted on driving, claiming his head felt better than ever and that he hadn't taken a pain pill for days. Amelia gave concise instructions and within minutes, they pulled up beside a two-story yellow house with white trim. The front yard was rimmed with a low white fence which in turn was bordered by a few flowers. Fluffy pink roses climbed a trellis on one corner of the house and three pillars supported an angled roof over a long porch. The front door was painted black with a large oval window.

"It looks like a nice place," Ryder said.

Standing beside him, Amelia nodded. "Your mother loved this house."

"Why did she and my father sell it?"

"It got to be too much for your father to keep up."

"Because of his heart?"

"You know about that?"

"Nina told me before they left. I think she felt guilty for abandoning me."

"Your mother is a wonderful woman."

"I wouldn't know," he said, and was surprised to hear the harshness in his voice. He cleared his throat, uncomfortable with the self-pity he'd been indulging in all morning. "But she certainly seems terrific," he added.

A small boy and a woman carrying a wicker basket came around the far side of the house. The woman paused by the roses as if to cut a few, but when she saw Ryder and Amelia, she crossed the lawn, the boy skipping ahead several feet.

"May I help you?" she called.

"We were just admiring your house," Ryder said.

The child reached the fence and immediately began climbing. His mother shouted, "Alex!" but with a playful glint, the boy kept going until he hoisted himself to the top horizontal support, balanced precariously for a fraction of a second, and began a tumble into the flower border.

Amelia gasped, the mother dropped her basket and sprinted, and Ryder, moving quickly, intercepted the fall. Hoisting the boy into his arms, he looked into brown eyes that were like his own.

The reality of Amelia's pregnancy was suddenly so poignant that he felt speechless. Someday soon, he would hold his child.

By now, the woman inside the fence was reaching out for her boy. Ryder handed the little guy over. "He's no worse for wear, but I'm afraid I scrunched a few of your flowers in my daring rescue attempt," he said.

The woman smiled. "With Alex around, it's a wonder I have any left. Thanks so much."

"Your house and yard are beautiful," Amelia said. Ryder looked at her. There had been a wistful tone to her voice. He reached for her hand which she only mildly tried to withdraw before giving up and leaving it firmly clenched in his hand where it belonged.

He suddenly wished he could give her a house like this one, with a yard and flowers and a place for their baby to play and grow. Going back to work now had a new purpose, one that dealt with the future as well as the past.

"I can't take much of the credit," the woman confided as she put the boy down. With a grin, he wrapped his plump arms around his mother's leg and stared at Amelia. Obviously, a child with good taste...

"The lady who lived here before me planted all the perennials and the roses and the trees in the back. She was a wonder in the garden."

"Yes," Ryder murmured.

"And you should see the interior. She and her husband

raised three boys here, but the house looks like it belongs in a magazine. At least it did until Alex came along."

Ryder suddenly looked toward the upstairs dormer. "Is there still a window seat up there with a hinged lid?"

She looked incredulous. "Why, yes."

Amelia's grip tightened. "Do you remember?"

"No more than the window seat. The lid is red."

"Yes, it is," the woman said. "How did you know?"

Ryder looked from one woman's eyes to the other. The mother was incredulous, Amelia was hopeful. He said, "I...I played here as a child."

"Did you know that one of the boys who used to live here died this past summer? Did you know him?"

"No, I didn't know him," Ryder said, a lump forming in his throat.

Patty, the receptionist at the OB clinic, took one look at Ryder and almost swooned. Amelia, who had failed in her quest to banish Ryder to a far corner while she signed in for her appointment, prepared herself for the humiliation that was certain to follow.

"You must be Mr. Enderling," Patty gushed.

Ryder, startled, mumbled, "Excuse me?"

Glancing now at Amelia, Patty added, "Mrs. Enderling, you never told me how handsome your husband is."

With a sigh, Amelia said, "Didn't I?"

Patty was staring at Ryder again. "What an exciting life you lead!" she gushed, clapping thin hands together beneath her chin. "Bangkok one week, Bora Bora the next. Paris, Istanbul, Tibet...oh, I've always wanted to travel like you do." She winked and added, "Guess I should have become an airline pilot instead of a receptionist, huh? Not much call for a receptionist on a commercial jetliner."

"I guess not," Ryder said.

The receptionist sat forward, eyes dancing. "Where are you off to next?"

Ryder blinked and said, "Uh—Casablanca."

"Oh, my gosh."

"I'll say hello to Humphrey Bogart for you."

The older woman erupted into giggles and shook her pencil at Ryder. "You're a tease, Mr. Enderling."

Amelia took a seat. Ryder, a smile toying with his lips, joined her.

"Mr. Enderling?" he said, sitting down.

"I should have warned you."

"Tibet? Bora Bora?"

"I can explain."

"Please, go right ahead."

"When I got here the first time, I realized I was a lot more conventional than I thought I was."

"So you created a husband?"

"When the receptionist mistook my father's wedding ring for my own, I went along with it." Amelia idly rotated the gold filigree band she wore on the middle finger of her left hand.

Lowering her voice, she added, "I told everyone my husband was a pilot which explained why he was never at these appointments with me. Little did I know Patty was harboring a life-long yen for adventure. She asks where you are every time I come in here and spreads it through the office. So, now I just keep you trotting around the globe, flying hither and yon."

Ryder said, "What were you going to do when the time came to deliver? Was I still going to be...away?"

Amelia stared at him for a few seconds while her mind raced. She hadn't planned on actually having the baby in Oregon, let alone Seaport, but she could hardly tell him that. Thank goodness she had never told anyone at the clinic that she was going to move out of state. At first, she'd planned to contact them once she got to Nevada, and then Ryder had had his accident and all her plans had been put on hold.

Now, she said, "I was going to cross that bridge when the time came."

"Hmm—"

The door opened and a nurse called out Amelia's name. "Mrs. Enderling? The doctor will see you now."

"I'll only be a few minutes," Amelia said, standing.

But Ryder stood, too. Looking down at her, he said, "I wouldn't miss this for the world."

"Ryder—"

"Just call me Mr. Enderling."

"I don't think—"

"When I held that little boy this morning, I realized how much I'm looking forward to our baby, Amelia. Don't deny me the privilege of sharing this with you. It means a lot to me."

She'd been trying to block out the way he had looked holding the child. How strong his arms were, the vast difference in size and color and texture between a three-year-old boy and a twenty-eight-year-old man. She'd never before seen Ryder even notice a child, let alone hold one, and it had softened her already spongy heart to witness the fleeting but tender moment when Ryder swooped the boy into his arms and stared into his eyes.

"Please," he added.

Short of making a scene, Amelia could see no way to stop him from coming with her. She was now officially drowning in that dreaded pool of confusion.

Amelia introduced Ryder to the doctor using his real last name. Lots of couples kept their own names nowadays, she figured, and there was no reason to lie when it wasn't necessary.

"You gained a few extra pounds," the doctor said as she examined Amelia's chart.

"I can't see how," Ryder said. "It doesn't seem to me that she eats very much."

"It's nothing to worry about, Mr. Hogan. Your wife was a little underweight when she began this pregnancy, so everything is well within bounds." As she measured Amelia's bulging abdomen, she glanced over her shoulder and added, "I hear you're flying to Casablanca next."

"News travels fast around here."

"Patty is our very own information highway. Of course, your life sounds pretty exciting to those of us working inside all day."

"It's not as exciting as it sounds," he said. "For one thing, it takes me away from Amelia. I worry about her when I'm...out of the country."

Amelia frowned. Where was he going with this dialogue?

After gentle prodding, the doctor rubbed gel onto Amelia's belly, but she turned around to face Ryder again. "It must be very difficult to be far away so often."

Amelia couldn't see Ryder's face—the doctor was in the way. She suspected he looked incredibly gorgeous and completely sincere, a deadly combination to any woman.

He said, "Yes, it is. Doctor, wouldn't you say that a woman in Amelia's condition needs her husband nearby?"

"Ideally, of course."

"I'm considering changing positions so that I'll be here in Seaport full-time from now on."

The doctor bathed Amelia with a glowing smile of approval. "Your husband's priorities are admirable."

"I'm a lucky woman," Amelia said dryly.

"Yes, you are. Oh, the stories I could tell you. But never mind, you're one of the lucky ones. It's always easier when there's a loving spouse to help."

Amelia grimaced and it wasn't just because of the pressure the doctor exerted while scooting the fetal stethoscope around on her tummy. Ryder was up to his old tricks, setting the groundwork for the argument she knew was forthcoming. She would say, I'm leaving your apartment as soon as Nina returns from California and that's that. And he would counter with, You heard the doctor. She said you should stay close by your loving husband.

At that, she would play her trump card and remind him that he wasn't really her husband.

The room fell silent except for the background noise of Amelia's blood swishing through her body. Occasionally, a thump erupted. The doctor glanced at Ryder again and said, "Sounds like we've got a soccer star in the making."

Ryder appeared at Amelia's side. Flat on her back, she couldn't tell just what parts of her anatomy the gown did and didn't conceal. She fought a tremendous urge to adjust her coverings, wondering what the doctor would think about a pregnant woman becoming shy around her devoted spouse. She felt naked and exposed and her cheeks flamed.

"Shouldn't we hear a heartbeat?" Ryder said.

"Sometimes the baby is against the back of the womb," the doctor said in a distracted voice. She pulled the paper gown down over Amelia's belly and helped her sit. Ryder stayed close by the examination table.

The doctor looked at both of them. "Amelia, you seem to be further along than I thought you were. I know you said you didn't want an ultrasound, but I really think we should schedule one and check things out. I won't divulge the sex of the baby if you don't want me to."

Ryder's voice sounded strained as he muttered, "Further along?"

Amelia knew he was doing the math and thinking about what she'd told him. If they'd had sex only one time, then further along meant the baby wasn't his. Trouble was, there had been no one else.

On top of everything else, was he now going to have to agonize over the possibility she was lying to him about his paternity? What could she possibly say or do that would convince him he was her child's father, short of waiting until the baby was born and demanding a blood test.

And then another thought struck her. If Ryder doubted he was this baby's father, would it be easier to leave?

But what about Jack and Nina?

What about her child's right to know his or her father?

What about Ryder?

And what about the truth?

Addressing the doctor, she mumbled, "If I'm further along, then this baby is the result of an immaculate conception."

Ryder rubbed his temple. If things had been different between them, she would look into his eyes and assure him that there was a mistake of some kind, that he needn't worry.

The doctor jotted a few notes in her folder and said, "Couples often miscalculate the date of conception. It's no big deal. I'm going to check with Patty to see if we can fit you in right away. Don't get dressed yet, Amelia.''

"Listen," Amelia began as the door closed behind the doctor. Ryder stilled her with a fingertip across her lips. Lowering his head, he gently kissed her cheek. Surprise quickly evaporated to a lightheaded faintness. The sudden need she felt to be close to him, to share all this with the only other person on the face of the earth who could begin to care as much as she did, to make him understand and trust her—all this caused her to melt against his strong body.

She allowed herself the luxury of feeling connected to him. After all the lonely doctor visits, after all the days and nights of telling and retelling herself she was independent and strong and didn't need—didn't even want—anyone's help, it was incredible to let go a little.

His arms encircled her with warmth.

"Don't worry," he said.

He was thinking about the absence of the baby's heartbeat. He couldn't feel his child doing gymnastics inside his body the way she could. She glanced up and said, "I'm not worried. Everything is fine."

"That's what I mean," he said, then lowering his face, he kissed her. Her heartbeat quadrupled as his lips pressed against hers. When he spoke next, it was a whisper. "No matter what, no matter...who, I'll stand by you."

"What!"

"It doesn't matter," he said, gently smoothing her hair away from her brow, his gaze intense and serious. "If you...lied about me being the father, you had a reason. It's okay."

"But, Ryder—"

"I understand," he said. "Trust me, it doesn't matter."

"But—"

He stilled further protests by kissing her again.

Chapter Eight

Though the doctor left nothing unexplained, Amelia paid her minimal attention.

Ryder stood next to her, his left hand resting on her right shoulder. He'd said he would stand by her through thick and thin, even if she carried someone else's baby. She wanted to strangle him and kiss him at the same time.

Then her focus shifted to the emerging image on the screen and the miracle of witnessing her first glimpse of her first child.

She heard Ryder's breath catch. "Is that...our baby?"

Amelia tore her attention away from the monitor to glance up at Ryder. He was staring beyond her, but perhaps feeling her gaze, he looked down, his eyes glistening.

A vise closed suddenly and decisively around Amelia's heart, twisting and squeezing until the pain brought tears to her own eyes. The burst of emotion must have showed, for Ryder leaned over and tenderly kissed her lips.

"Our baby," he said again, and she knew exactly what he meant.

Their baby. She knew he was the father. He did not— not for sure, anyway—and yet here he was, willing and anxious to assume all responsibility.

How could he have changed so much!

For the first time, the enormity of whisking away Ryder's baby—this Ryder's baby—hit her like a brick in the face.

Amelia's gaze went back to the monitor, back to the black and white form of her child. The only shape she was sure of was a hand. "Which is it?" she asked the doctor. "I want to know if it's a boy or a girl."

The doctor looked closely at the screen, then from Ryder to Amelia. "I was wrong," she said. "You're not further along. You're right on schedule."

"Then is he or she a large baby?"

With a smile, the doctor outlined shapes on the monitor with the tip of her pencil. "I seem to remember that twins run in your family, Dad."

Ryder and Amelia looked at each other again as the meaning of the doctor's observation sank in.

Amelia finally sputtered, "Are you saying—"

"There are two babies, yes, that's what I'm saying. Two perfect babies. It's a little hard to tell, but I'd say twin girls."

"Twins!" Ryder gasped.

Astounded, bewildered, a little afraid and absolutely stunned, Amelia couldn't stop staring at the monitor. The images blurred as her eyes filled. "Twins," she murmured, her heart swelling with emotion.

"Good thing there are four arms between us," Ryder said softly. Amelia glanced back at his face. Tears rolled down his cheeks and he wiped them away. She yearned to tell him not to bother, that no man had ever looked half as desirable as he did at that moment, face damp, dark eyes pools of wonder, a startled smile firmly in place.

I love you, Amelia thought, taking care the words didn't find their way to her lips, tucking them away safely in her heart. For better or worse, this was the man she loved. No matter how frightening it was, no matter how foolish to give her love to a man who wouldn't want it once he regained his past, it didn't matter.

What did matter was the gut-wrenching certainty that if she waited much longer, she might never find the courage to leave him.

One week later than anticipated, the message Amelia had both been waiting for and dreading was finally on the answering machine. Jack and Nina were home.

Ryder immediately called his parents.

"Come to dinner," he said into the receiver, which startled her. For weeks, he'd wanted little or nothing to do with his family, and now he was inviting them over.

Thank goodness, she thought with an internal sigh of relief. He needs to reconnect with them. He needs to have someone in Seaport he feels close to besides me.

"No, I insist," he said. Apparently, Nina was as surprised by Ryder's sudden hospitality as she was.

After a lengthy pause, he added, "No, I still don't remember much. I know, I wish it would all come back, too."

He grinned at Amelia who managed a wan smile.

"As a matter of fact," he said after another pause, "we have a surprise of our own. Okay, we'll see you in a couple of hours."

He faced Amelia. "You don't mind, do you?"

"Of course not."

"I just want to tell them about the babies."

He was still wearing an invincible grin that ate away at her heart, but she made herself nod. For days she had skirted the real issues that lay between them. She had even considered selling the Nevada house and buying one in Seaport so Ryder and the babies could be close to one another. Truth of the matter was, she didn't know what to do.

Whatever it was, it had to be said or done soon. Though she wanted to believe differently, she feared that she and the children would go from being a light in his eyes to a burden he would resent with every breath he took. Tomorrow, she would have to be honest with him. She would assure him he could visit his babies as often as he liked and she would try not to dwell on the fact that his visits would inevitably taper off as he gradually recovered.

He had known there was a book by his reading chair, a rope swing at the river, a red window seat at his boyhood home. The memories were slowly beginning to surface.

"Amelia?"

She glanced up to find him staring at her.

"You okay?"

"Of course."

"Good. Nina said they have a surprise for me. I bet it's nothing compared with our news."

Rising, Amelia said, "If we're having company, I'd better go to the store and buy something to eat."

"Never fear, I'll take care of everything."

She leaned against the counter and watched Ryder search the spartan cupboards. "Wait a second, you don't cook."

"That's what you think." He produced a small flat can and added triumphantly, "Aha! Anchovies. I thought I saw a can in here." He checked the contents of the refrigerator, mumbling to himself.

This was yet another new facet. Ryder cooking?

He took her hands and led her into the living room. He kept staring at her as though she was a treasure. It made Amelia feel rotten.

"Twins," he said, gazing into her eyes.

"Yes—"

"Are you pleased, Amelia?"

"Pleased? That's too weak a word. I'm dazzled. I can hardly wait."

"You're going to need another one of those little white things to embroider."

"I don't know if I want to dress them alike," she said. If her girls were as identical as Ryder and Rob, they would need to maintain their separate identities. She would make sure they did. "I think I'll do something different for each of them," she added. "I need to learn to knit."

He wrapped her in his arms and she allowed herself the pleasure of resting her head against his chest. His heart thumped reassuringly beneath her cheek.

"I can't begin to tell you what all this means to me," he said softly. "Two babies...my daughters. I have a family now, one I'll know from the beginning, children with whom to create memories. New memories. You're not only a link with my past, sweetheart, you're the bridge to my future. I owe you everything—"

"No, Ryder—"

"Yes."

She tore her gaze from his face. "I want you to know that you are the father. There was no one else, just you."

"You told me that already."

"You said it didn't matter if I lied. I didn't lie."

He held her away and stared at her. "I know. I'm sorry. It's just that when I look at you, I see the world, Amelia. I see all the opportunities, all the possibilities. It really doesn't matter if the babies are mine because they're yours. That's what I was trying to say."

She felt tears puddling in her eyes again.

His gaze grew soft and enveloped her like comforting twilight after a long, hard day. When his lips touched hers, she closed her eyes and drifted with him on a current of sensation that was all the more moving because it was bittersweet. She ran her hands across his wonderful face, into his silky hair, as he held her so tight she could scarcely breathe, and still the kisses went on and on, mesmerizing her.

She didn't protest when he lifted her in his arms and carried her to the couch, sinking down with her onto the plush cushions. He stared at her for so long, she began to wonder if another memory was poking its way through the haze. She hoped not. She wanted him to lie down with her and love away the pain that adoring him created.

He slowly stood.

"Why don't you rest while I do the shopping?" His voice was husky, his gaze impenetrable.

Then he was gone in a flash.

She closed her eyes, resting her hands on her abdomen, cradling her children in the only way possible. As much as she longed for the moment she would gaze into their eyes and know they were hers forever, she dreaded the day she lost Ryder. One of the babies kicked, or perhaps both, and she smiled through her tears.

"First, you put in the seasonings," Ryder said as he ground peppercorns into a wooden bowl he'd found in a cupboard above the refrigerator. "Then you mash up a couple of garlic cloves with your fork and add an anchovy filet."

Sitting on a stool, Amelia made a face.

"What's the matter, you don't like anchovies?"

"No."

"Don't worry, you won't even taste it," he said as he added a dollop of Dijon mustard. He moved to the pot of boiling water and carefully dropped in an egg for a few seconds. The coddled yolk went into the bowl.

"It's raw!" Amelia said.

"No it's not. It's cooked enough to kill the germs. Do you think I would risk the health of you and our children?"

He knew he was grinning. He just couldn't seem to stop. This whole twin thing was a miracle, no more, no less. He had thought the euphoria might wear off. Ha!

Now he whisked the ingredients with his fork, blending in the oil.

"Do you need help?" Amelia asked.

As it was the second time she'd asked, he decided she wanted something to do so he set her to work breaking apart romaine lettuce. The croutons were made, the Parmesan cheese grated. Add the lettuce, toss judiciously, and presto, the first course. The chicken was marinating, the rice cooking, and since no one seemed to drink alcohol, he'd prepared a pitcher of iced tea.

Right on time, the doorbell rang. Amelia ushered in his parents, hugging them each, her gray eyes looking worried as they lingered on his father's haggard face. She told them over and over again how happy she was to see them, how glad she was that they were home. He hoped her enthusiasm helped make up for his reserve.

His mother hugged him, then studied his face. "That scar makes you look distinctive," she said at last.

His hand automatically went to his cheek. "Thanks."

"Quite dashing. But you need a haircut, honey. I believe your last one was right before Philip got married. You and Rob went together...before the...accident..."

Her voice petered out as her eyes became bright. Ryder decided the best thing would be to move right along to dinner, so he immediately seated everyone at the table and passed around the Caesar salad.

"This is delicious," his mother said, her equilibrium recovered. "I didn't know you could cook."

"Rob was always the one who fooled around in the kitchen," Jack said. His pale skin, pinched face and hunched figure spoke volumes about the stress of their trip, and Ryder's heart went out to his father.

"Maybe I'll adopt some of my brother's aptitudes," Ryder said, intrigued by the idea. He'd read up on twins during the last few weeks and he knew they often shared the same interests. Then he confessed that the real credit belonged to a cooking show he'd watched on television while Amelia napped. He'd copied the menu from beginning to end.

He didn't tell them that making the salad had seemed familiar or that he had modified the recipe, switching from olive oil to safflower oil because he *knew* that in this dish, the former would leave a taste on the back of his tongue.

How could he know that? Had someone at the Mona Lisa told him?

For once, he had an appetite, though Amelia barely picked at her food which concerned him—heck, she was eating for three now. But he kept his observations to himself. She'd been quiet all evening and he wondered if it had been as tough on her as it had been on him when he'd gallantly left to do the shopping instead of making love to her like every particle of his body yearned to.

He wanted her so much it hurt, but he didn't want her until she wanted him for more than one night. She said she didn't love him. That what they'd once had was over. He didn't want to believe her. Anyway, there was so much at stake now.

He'd forgotten about dessert, but no one seemed to care. While he piled the dishes in the sink, he heard the door close and went out to the living room to find his mother absent. Amelia and his dad sat side by side on the sofa, both looking preoccupied with their own thoughts.

As a dinner party, this one lacked a certain buoyancy!

All that changed a second later when the front door opened and a small scruffy dog with two bright black eyes dragged Nina into the room. "We brought you Rob's terrier!" she cried as she held on to the red leash.

Jack said, "That dog is nuts."

"He is not," Nina insisted as she patted the mutt who grudgingly quieted down. Ryder held out a hand and was rewarded with a snarl. He inched closer and the dog snapped at him. Great dog for a man with babies on the way, he thought, wondering how to tell his mother he couldn't keep the animal. Sure, part of him wanted a part of Rob, but preferably one that didn't bite.

"That's odd, isn't it? You being twins, I would have thought Socrates would adore you like he adored Rob. The neighbors said they played fetch."

Ryder smiled. What fit of whimsy made Rob name a dog Socrates?

"The neighbors also said Rob only had the animal a few weeks," Jack added.

Amelia's attempt to pet the animal resulted in more snaps.

"He's young," Nina said as she smoothed the dog's spiky fur.

"He's a twit," Jack insisted. He held up a bandaged finger and added, "A twit with a big name and even bigger teeth."

"Well," Ryder said, "he sure likes you...Mom."

Nina's smile this time seemed more genuine. Ryder tried to remember if he'd called her mom since the accident and was pretty sure he hadn't. It must have broken her heart to have her son in the room but out to lunch.

So to speak.

"Maybe I should keep him myself," Nina mused. "It would be like having a little piece of Rob. I could call him Socks for short."

Ryder nodded, relieved. "I'm sure Rob would want you to have...Socks."

"Do you think so?"

"Of course." There was something he'd been wanting to say to his parents, but had been afraid to broach. It concerned his accident. It seemed to him every time he mentioned anything remotely connected to that day everyone froze. Summoning his resolve, he blurted it out. "I haven't told you yet how sorry I am about Rob."

The tears rolled now, but Ryder continued.

"It had to be horrible for both of you. Of course, I can't remember the details and I know the doctor has asked you not to talk to me about it, but I just want you to know that I'm sorry Rob died. I'm sorry you have to try to rebuild me. I'm just sorry the blasted accident ever happened."

Nina looked at Jack, Jack looked at Amelia, and Amelia stared at her feet. Ryder felt as though he'd just committed a huge faux pas that had struck everyone dumb. Quickly, he added, "I take it you settled all of Rob's affairs?"

Jack recovered first. "He had a little office down there with a partner," he said. "Julia is six months pregnant, so she'll have to take some leave and without Rob—well, she's afraid the whole thing will go under."

"At least we sold his house," Nina added, apparently relieved to talk about concrete things. "We had to take a huge loss on it, but that's okay. All we really wanted was to get home." A sidelong glance at Jack followed this comment. "Anyway, besides a few bequests to his friends, Rob left everything to us. We boxed up some of his stuff for you and Philip, stuff we thought Rob would want you to have..."

She stopped abruptly, her lips trembling.

"Ryder has been so anxious for you to return," Amelia said. "Has he told you he's been remembering little things? Not much, but it's a start."

"That's wonderful," Nina said as she blotted her eyes with a tissue.

"I know how impatient you must be to spend lots of time together...as a family," Amelia continued. "I bet some concentrated time with you and Jack..."

Jack coughed into his hand. It sounded innocent to Ryder, but Nina reacted as though it was a tsunami warning.

Ryder was touched by his mother's devotion but alarmed by her concern. Apparently, so was Amelia, for she looked from one to the other with huge eyes that seemed to see things that were invisible to him.

"About tomorrow..." she said tentatively.

"Not tomorrow," Nina interrupted. "Jack has a doctor's appointment and then he needs rest. You two young people carry on as you have been. Apparently, it's working.''

Ryder realized they were leaving. Reaching down, he took Amelia's hand and pulled her to her feet. "Wait. Before you go, there's something we want to tell you.''

As he looked at all three faces, it occurred to him that he had a lot to do and not much time in which to do it. He needed to help his parents in whatever way he could. He needed to reclaim his career and look for a house with a yard for his daughters. And most of all, he needed to convince Amelia that she wanted to stay by his side, in his home—not across town, but here with him, where she belonged.

He had to convince her because the truth was that without her, none of the rest of it mattered.

Ryder took a deep breath and entered the remodeled Victorian where up until the accident he had spent his work days. He hadn't announced that he was returning today because he wanted a few minutes of privacy. He was hoping the familiarity of the place would jar loose a flood of memories.

Or even one memory—hey, at this point, he wasn't picky.

Steep stairs rose to the right of the large lobby, a small elevator beneath them. Directly to the left was a desk, behind which sat an attractive woman with red hair and lips to match. She didn't look at him, probably because her attention was directed at the two people standing in front of the desk. One was another woman, a trim brunette in a very classy black suit. The other was a middle-age man with a balding head. Though his back was to Ryder, he had a belligerent stance. It was he who was speaking in a deep rumble.

Ryder blocked out the people and looked around. He saw cases of books, a few well-cared-for plants, thick carpets, oak furniture. The paint was fresh, the walls covered with silk paper. Brass ornaments gleamed, glass sparkled. It all looked less intimidating than a skyscraper, a coat of expensive civility overlaying legal efficiency.

It didn't cause the slightest stir in his head. Not a flicker, nothing.

He heard his name and discovered all three strangers were looking at him in varying degrees of shock.

The man strode forward, hand outstretched. Ryder wondered if this guy was Goodman, Todd or Flanders. He didn't look like a lawyer, whatever that meant.

"Ryder," the man said, grasping Ryder's hand. "You old son of a gun. It's good to see you, boy. Hey, I won't lie, it threw me for a loop when they said you'd had an accident and wouldn't be handling my case, but Samantha did a grand job." A broad wink was followed with the comment, "She tore that wacko veteran apart. It was truly a thing of beauty. Looks like you'll have to share your bonus with her!"

Ryder tried to look as if he knew what the man was talking about. The brunette sniffed. "I don't want a penny. We all know who the brains was behind your…defense."

"You two kids work it out," the man said, and with another wink, left.

The brunette looked at Ryder like she might a flattened toad on a highway. The redhead licked her lips. She reminded him of Lily and the look in her green eyes said she knew him way better than he knew her.

Of course, that wouldn't be much of a trick.

So, one didn't trust him and one had the hots for him. Apparently, he had been just as "charming" at work as in his personal life. A threatening throb in his temples warned him that his brain was approaching overload. Again.

The brunette finally said, "You don't have any idea who we are, not me or Gail or even Kurt Dalton, do you?"

He cracked his first real smile. "Not a clue."

"I'm Samantha Cooke, your trusty co-worker. I'm the one who ran with the Dalton case when you were... incapacitated. Kurt Dalton, by the way, is the man who just oozed out of here. And this is Gail Bascomb, our receptionist."

Gail said, "That scar looks wicked, Ryder."

Samantha Cooke shook her head. "Miles Flanders will want to see you. Top of the stairs, first door on the right. Or you can take the elevator."

"The stairs will be fine," he said.

Miles Flanders looked as though he ran two miles every day before breakfast and played tennis on the weekends. He had the stare of a wolf on the prowl. "So you still don't remember the...accident?" he said at last.

"No."

"Nothing?"

Ryder shook his head. "Why are you asking?"

After a moment of scrutiny, Flanders shrugged. "Just curious. Never been around anyone with amnesia before. I'll be blunt. You're a valuable asset at Goodman, Todd and Flanders. You have a way of turning a no-win situation around. The groundwork you did on the Dalton case was inspired. But without your memory... Take some time, Ryder. You have excellent health benefits."

"I wasn't suggesting I go into the courtroom tomorrow," Ryder said. "I can remember studying law, but I have no memory of practicing it. My hope was that the familiar routine of the office would speed things up.''

"We farmed out your cases after the accident. Billings took the Poe murder case and Cooke went to trial with Dalton. She used your game plan and won an acquittal."

"So she mentioned," Ryder said.

Flanders's eyebrows inched upward. "You've seen her?"

"She and Dalton were downstairs when I got here. I get the feeling she's not my biggest fan."

"Well, after the way you two—"

Ryder held up his hand. "Please, don't say another word. I don't want to know. I don't remember and to tell you the truth, I don't want to."

Flanders emitted a short bark of laughter. "Well, she wasn't thrilled with Dalton. She made no pretense of that. Like I always say, heaven save us from an idealistic lawyer."

Ryder didn't know how to respond. He thought of the way Samantha had said Dalton "oozed" out of the office and how she'd then looked at Ryder as though he was some kind of road kill. Was it all personal or was there something more?

"You hang around, study in the basement library if you want, use your desk, review past litigation. But no new cases until you're one hundred percent. Deal?"

Ryder shook Flanders's hand. "Deal. One more thing, is Gail my secretary?" He sincerely hoped she wasn't.

"No. I'll get Vincent to show you around."

Ryder waited in Flanders's office until a man with a brown buzz cut appeared and ushered him downstairs. Vincent was blatantly curious about Ryder's amnesia and asked as many questions as he answered. The tour ended in Ryder's corner office. Before he closed the door, Vincent asked if there was anything Ryder wanted.

"I didn't see a coffee machine."

"It's in the back. You want a cup? Black, right?"

"Yes, black. And I'd like to see the Dalton file."

"Sure thing. You do know Samantha won that case?"

"Yeah, I know. I just want to review my notes."

With a nod, Vincent was gone.

Exercises done, Amelia put her mat away and sank down on the sofa. It was weird, but ever since she'd learned she was carrying twins, her belly seemed twice as big as before. She could swear she was walking funny, too.

"It's all in my head," she said aloud but it wasn't. It was all in her mid-section which was growing larger by the microsecond. Two babies! "You guys have my permission to be petite," she murmured, thinking ahead to their births. She smiled. Her life was as confusing as ever, but still she smiled.

Patty had signed her up for childbirth classes and a tour of the hospital before they left the doctor's office. Ryder had eagerly expressed his desire to accompany her.

She still hadn't said a word to him about Nevada. This morning, she had sipped her coffee and tried to think how to broach the subject while he ignored his grapefruit and ate his cereal. Unfortunately, no brilliant idea had presented itself, so in the end she told him they needed to talk that evening. Good old procrastination.

Truth was, she had counted on Nina to swoop in and rescue the day. Now Amelia had to face the fact that Nina's priority was Jack and would be for quite a while.

So how long did Amelia put her plans on hold? How long *could* she?

Addressing her children, she said, "I won't go until your daddy has recovered enough of his memory to be independent. Don't worry, I won't leave him in the lurch." The thought immediately occurred to her that he already was independent. He drove, shopped, cooked, went to work. He didn't need her.

So, she should screw up her courage, gently tell him her plans...and pack her bags.

She was still sprawled on the sofa, trying to make two aqua knitting needles do something creative with a ball of pink yarn when the door opened and Ryder entered. He didn't see her immediately, and for one second she thought he must have remembered something unpleasant because of the awful expression on his face. And then she realized he looked tired beyond endurance. Tired and sick at heart.

Now what? she thought with dread.

Her next thought catapulted her heart into her throat.

Had he remembered the accident? Had he remembered that he was behind the wheel, that he was responsible for Rob's death? Had someone said something that triggered—

As if sensing her presence, he turned just then. His face immediately relaxed and a smile appeared.

"You're a sight for sore eyes," he said, his smooth exterior falling into place as he advanced.

"What's wrong?" she said, laying aside the needles, yarn and instruction booklet. Eventually, she began to struggle to her feet. Ryder grabbed her hands and helped.

"Nothing."

"Liar."

Shaking his head, he said, "It's nothing really."

"Did someone say...something to you at work?"

"What do you mean?"

She blinked. "Well, you know, people talk."

He stared at her a second as though trying to guess what she thought people would talk about. Then he said, "No one said much of anything. Everyone was very nice. Distant, but nice. They treated me like a laboratory animal which was okay because that's exactly how I felt."

"Then—"

He kissed her forehead. "You look beautiful today. Very fetching in your exercise clothes."

"I'm a regular femme fatale and you're trying to change the subject."

"What makes you so sure?"

"I saw your face when you came through the door."

He sighed deeply and ran a hand through his longish hair. "I don't want to bother you, Amelia. You need to conserve your energy for yourself and our babies."

"Go ahead, bother me," she said lightly, trying not to show how stunned she was that Ryder would think of her needs before his own.

But why should she be stunned? The man standing before her wasn't selfish, at least not now. If she was constantly mixing up the past man with the present man, what must it be like for him?

He said, "Didn't you have something you wanted to tell me when I got home? Here I am."

"It can wait."

Still he hesitated, but she tilted her head and narrowed her eyes, gestures she'd used in the past to coax his feelings from him. Finally, he said, "Today I had a lesson in what it means to be Ryder Hogan."

"And that means?"

"It means I got an up close and personal view of the kind of man I am."

"You're talking in circles."

He shook his head. The unease was back, the discouragement, the distaste. It showed in his mouth, in his eyes and in his shoulders and made Amelia long to comfort him.

She ran a hand up his arm until her fingers caressed his cheek. "What did you discover about yourself today?"

"I discovered I'm without ethics. I discovered I will do almost anything for money. I'm a shyster, Amelia. There's nothing about my career to be proud of. If it wasn't for you and our babies, there would be no point in regaining my memory."

He wrapped her in his arms and rested his cheek against the top of her head. "And now I know why you want to leave me," he mumbled in her hair.

Amelia allowed herself to melt against him. For so long, she had needed and wanted him and he'd been unapproachable. At that moment, he was everything she had ever wanted, warm and vulnerable, aware of his shortcomings, yet rock solid in his resolve, even if he had yet to discover it. It was there, she knew it was.

And at that moment, leaving him was the last thing on Amelia's mind.

Chapter Nine

The cool wind scattered ribbons of seaweed across the beach and blew the tops off the waves. Amelia plucked strands of hair from her mouth and wished she'd thought to wear a jacket with a hood. When Ryder had told her he wanted to take a walk, she'd assumed he meant around the block, not down to the ocean.

He seemed mesmerized as he gazed toward the vast horizon. The sun was low, streaking the sky with orange and purple, flooding his face with the warm hues of approaching fall. Finally, he took a deep breath, shoved his hands in his pockets, and smiled at her. His hair whipped away from his forehead and though there was still a trace of uneasiness in his eyes, there was also a glimpse of tranquillity, as though he'd reached a decision.

"Have I always loved the ocean?" he asked.

The truth was, he preferred crowded restaurants and noisy nightclubs. But that was an old truth, an irrelevant truth. Amelia said, "The point is, do you love it now?"

"Yes," he said without pause. "It's revitalizing. It makes my problems seem relatively insignificant."

He took her hand and they walked along the surf. She concentrated on the feel of the hard-packed sand beneath her feet, the smell of seaweed and salt, the overhead cries of the gulls. She tried to ignore the feel of his fingers gripping hers, as though she represented a lifeline. She was dying of curiosity, wondering what in the world could have happened at his office to rattle him so.

She wasn't sure how long they walked, only that the elements went from chilly to freezing, from windy to oppressive as the fog crept down the beach, one step ahead of the night.

Amelia shivered. Ryder stopped and draped an arm over her shoulders, but it did little to reduce her trembling.

"I've been here before," he said.

"You remember this beach?"

He looked down at her. "Have you ever really thought about what a memory is? Is it just an impression, stored like a photo in a box, or more like a video on a shelf? I mean, I can remember yesterday's sandwich in a dozen different ways, from the taste of the bread to the crunch of the sprouts to the smell of the tomato to how it looked on the plate. But my memories, such as they are, are prioritized by past experiences, by what I think is important or what strikes a chord in my head or heart. Memories are subjective, and basically, when you come right down to it, they're fickle and unreliable and misleading and yet, perhaps, they're a truer indication of what matters to us than actual facts.

"I can't tell you when, but I've stood on this beach before. I found peace then, just like I'm finding it now."

Amelia took a chance. "What happened today, Ryder?"

Looking right at her, he said, "I shouldn't be discussing this with you. Ethically, it's not right. But if I don't tell someone, I'll go nuts. And you're the someone I want to tell."

Amelia's shudder this time had nothing to do with the cold. There was an ominous tone to his voice as well as to his words. She said, "You can tell me anything, Ryder. What is it?"

He withdrew his arm. "Do you remember a fire in Seaport about eight months ago? It burned down an old warehouse."

"Vaguely. Didn't someone die?"

"Yes, a homeless man who had taken to slipping through a broken window and sleeping on the second floor."

"I think I read in the paper that the owner of the building was accused of starting the fire. An insurance scam maybe. I don't remember the trial, though."

"That's probably because it began a couple of days after my accident. Turns out the owner is a guy named Kurt Dalton. I discovered today he was my client. After my accident, the case was reassigned to another lawyer in the firm and she won an acquittal by using the data I'd collected. Anyway, it all seemed kind of odd so today I reviewed my notes."

It was twilight and she could barely make out his features. She whispered, "What did you find?"

He rubbed his forehead. "There was a witness who swore he saw Dalton in the building that night, but Dalton had an alibi. The witness was a veteran with a history of stress-related issues. Apparently, he had a breakdown twenty-five years ago when half his men got caught in a fire and burned to death.

"It appears I dug around in this guy's past and decided he'd be easy to crack. I lined up all his shrinks, his two ex-wives, his three kids.... My stand-in used these people to discredit him. He broke, right on the stand."

"But—"

"There's more. In the file, in a separate envelope, I found a newspaper article written by a reporter who was doing a human interest piece about a soup kitchen two blocks from Dalton's building. A few minutes before the fire started, this guy took a picture of the kitchen from across the street. That picture was printed with the article in the people section. There's a blue circle drawn around one of the cars parked in front of the place. I guess I drew the circle. Using a magnifying glass, you can see the car has a dented fender which must be what originally caught my eye, but you can also read the license plate."

Amelia was lost. Teeth chattering, she whispered, "So?"

Ryder took off his suit jacket and slipped it around her shoulders, enveloping her in its musky warmth. "So, I couldn't help but wonder why that article was in there and why I'd circled the car. Then I noticed I'd written Dalton's name on the back of the envelope."

"What does the car—"

"It's Dalton's car. His kid banged it up the night before the fire. I checked. The photo was taken two blocks east, fifteen minutes before the alarm was pulled. Dalton wasn't at a dinner party with his girlfriend's family like they all said he was."

"He was downtown, close to his building."

"Yes. Which means Dalton lied about his whereabouts that night and, worse, I knew he lied. This is the third building he's owned that has burned to the ground. A watchman died in the first fire, but no one has ever been able to pin that or anything else on Dalton, so it couldn't be introduced in court—the jury didn't even know. It means Dalton's responsible for the death of a man whose only crime was looking for a dry spot to sleep. And it means that I'm the kind of lawyer who knows the truth and hides it.''

Searching for some way to ease the pain in his eyes, Amelia said, ''I'll play devil's advocate. Isn't that just doing your job? Unpleasant as it may be, isn't that what you're supposed to do? Couldn't the prosecution have found the same pictures and produced their own doctors if they'd been as smart as you?''

''Maybe it makes me a good attorney,'' Ryder said slowly, ''but tearing apart a veteran so a sleazeball like Kurt Dalton can walk free—well, that doesn't make me a good man and isn't that ultimately more important?''

''Yes,'' Amelia said quietly. ''Of course.''

She could feel him staring at her. At last he added, ''You're still cold.''

Pulling the jacket closer she said, ''I'm okay.''

''It was selfish of me to drag you down here.''

''No—''

''But you came along and you didn't protest. You never protest, Amelia. From the very beginning, you've been willing to go along with whatever I suggest, putting my needs ahead of your own. You're an amazing woman.''

''Ryder—''

''An amazing woman,'' he repeated, wrapping his arms around her. It was just about impossible to control her emotions when he touched her. She was trying to reconcile this Ryder with the man she had dated months before. While this Ryder continually impressed her with his thoughtfulness and compassion, memories of the way he'd once treated her kept rearing their ugly head.

How horrible that must be for him!

"You're trembling," he said.

"So are you."

His head lowered, and by the time he kissed her, she was breathless. He didn't stop with her mouth. Cupping her chin, he touched his lips to her cheeks and the hollow of her throat, her ears, her eyelids, her forehead. By the time he claimed her mouth again, she was damn near faint and so alarmed at herself that she wrenched away and immediately began to walk away. She was aware of him behind her, following, but not protesting.

His sensitivity and humanity made her love him all the more.

And then it came to her. Why was she fighting him? He was honest and kind, as well as charming and sexy. He was the kind of man she had always wanted. Why couldn't she accept that this new Ryder was the genuine article?

Ryder spent several afternoons that week at his office. Upon reviewing his cases, he reached a disturbing conclusion—his career was a veneer of decency covering a mass of compromise. No way around it.

He thought of his old teacher, Kendra Platt, and her blatant disapproval. At the time he'd thought her cruel, but now—

He would have to change. He would have to make retribution and in the future, he would have to conduct himself with honor. He had a feeling his days at Goodman, Todd and Flanders were numbered. He needed to find himself, and for some reason that led him to his parents' home.

They were obviously surprised to see him, but warmly welcomed him into their living room. Socrates growled and snapped until his father locked the dog in the kitchen.

Along with a wedding picture of Philip and Sara, Ryder found two pictures of himself hanging on the wall. Then it dawned on him that they weren't both of him. One was of Rob.

"Tell me about myself," he asked as the three of them sat down on comfortable furniture that looked so old he might have sat on it a million times.

"Oh, my," Nina said, sliding a long glance at Jack.

"Listen," he said, grasping his mother's hands, "don't give me some pretty picture. I'll make it easy for you. I know I'm a selfish man. I know I haven't been a good son. I know I compromise my values. But I also know I love Amelia and that I will make a damn fine father, and that for some reason, I've changed from the man I was before that accident. I'm hoping that you can help give me a sense of who I was as a child, as a boy. It might matter. Does this make any sense at all?"

Nina nodded, her eyes glistening with tears. Ryder had addressed her because she was obviously the stronger of his parents, so it surprised him when his father was the one who spoke.

"You and Rob were great little boys," he said, running a wrinkled hand through his graying hair. "Rob was the quiet one, you were rambunctious. I won't deny that you and I went around and around a few times, because you were headstrong and stubborn, too, but I always admired you, son. You knew what you wanted and you went after it."

"You always had a millions friends," Nina said. "I

can't tell you how many parties we held at the old house for you boys. Rob tended to go with one girl at a time, but you used to tell me that life was short and you intended on playing the field. That's why we were so pleased when you started going with Amelia."

"She's the best thing that ever happened to you," his father said.

Ryder nodded. "I agree."

"She's adorable," Nina added. "She looks soft, but she's strong and so very compassionate. She's going to make a wonderful mother. And a wonderful wife."

Ryder stared into his mother's eyes. She was hoping he would confirm this statement. He wanted to tell her the idea was fine with him but that he suspected Amelia might not agree. He hedged by saying, "Amelia is one of a kind."

"You were always special to me," Nina said. "Don't get me wrong, I loved all three of my boys. Philip was so athletic, Rob was sensitive and funny, you had the devil in you. We used to talk late into the night, you and I."

"What did we talk about?"

"Oh, everything and nothing. Books—you and Rob were such avid readers. Ideas. People. Everything."

Ryder tried to broach his next question in such a way that she could answer him without worrying that she was saying something hurtful. He said, "I didn't come around much once I got to be an adult. I'm sorry."

The smile on her face touched a corner of his heart. She placed her hand over his. "You were so busy, Ryder. Always busy. There was never a dull moment in your social life."

"I think what you liked most was the conquest of making…friends,'' his father added. ''Not the ongoing work of keeping a relationship viable.''

''Seems I was shallow and something of an opportunist,'' Ryder said. ''I think this horrible accident has changed all that. I think the accident has finally brought home what's important to me. I know I was afraid of making a commitment before. I'm not now.''

His parents both smiled at him and he realized that no matter what kind of son he'd been in the last few years, these two people loved him. They loved what he was once, what he was now, what he would become in the future. Just as he would love his daughters. Unrestricted, without boundaries.

Ryder felt his eyes fill with tears he wouldn't shed. In some indefinable way, the whole conversation sounded like a eulogy.

Maybe that was what it was.

''Thanks,'' he told them both, taking one of their hands in each of his.

''I don't know if we helped—''

''You helped,'' he assured them, and in some way, they had. For the first time since this ordeal began, he felt as though Nina and Jack were his parents.

At Nina's request, Philip and he each took a half-dozen boxes of Rob's things to their respective homes. It seemed sacrilegious to Ryder to look through them when he couldn't even remember Rob, so he stacked them in his bedroom for a later day.

And as the days passed, tiny things began to come back to him.

When he'd needed cuff links, he knew to look in a small wooden box on top of his dresser. The silver disks set in gold had seemed familiar, and he'd run his thumb across them before dressing. He would bet a million dollars he'd done the same thing a dozen times before.

He didn't say a word to Amelia. Her biggest fear seemed to be that he would revert into the monster from yesteryear. No reason to worry her unduly, not as long as his memory was returning in such sporadic, uneventful ways.

Like the blue scarf. He'd seen it in the front window of a shop near his office and he'd known immediately it was Amelia's favorite color. Right there on the edge of his brain was a memory of Amelia happy in blue. Cornflower blue, the clerk had called it, and he'd bought the scarf on the spot.

It was in his pocket now, wrapped in tissue. Tonight, he'd give it to her.

But first, he had a two o'clock appointment down at police headquarters to talk to the officer who had been first on the scene at the Dalton fire. The trial was over, but there was the not-so-small matter of insurance fraud. Before Ryder did anything, however, he was determined to reinvestigate the case from the beginning.

It took an hour for someone to get around to telling him that due to an emergency the appointment would be rescheduled. Ryder tempered his frustration with the knowledge he would have more time with Amelia.

He was walking down the hall when he recognized a lanky, gray-haired man staring at him from the doorway of an office. Detective Hill, in the flesh, and by the challenge in his eyes, still combative.

"Well, well," Hill said. "What are you doing here?"

"I had an appointment," Ryder said, instantly on guard.

"If your memory has returned, then I'm the one you

should be talking with, and I don't recall having an appointment with you.''

He knew Hill had been asking around about him, but he'd repressed his unease with that knowledge. Now it came stampeding back. "Why...what is it you want?"

Hill's jaw was as tightly clenched as his fists. "Listen," he said, eyes narrowed. "You may be fooling all the doctors, but you and I know you were the one behind the wheel. You were the one who was drunk. You were the one responsible for the crash. Maybe I'll never be able to prove it, thanks to that damn orderly who messed things up at the lab, but we all know you killed your brother.''

Startled beyond speech, Ryder stared into Hill's eyes. What he saw there was worse than what Hill had said, because who better than he, a trial lawyer, knew that words could be twisted, words could be used as weapons?

What he saw in Hill's eyes was the truth....

"The truth, Amelia."

She stared at him. He looked devastated. She suspected he already knew the truth.

"I went to the library after Hill told me," he said, pacing the living room. "I looked up accounts of the accident.''

"Ryder—"

"Hill's right. I was behind the wheel. I killed Rob."

"Ryder—"

He stopped pacing and stared at her. "You know the funny thing, Amelia? It doesn't surprise me. Everything I've learned about myself makes this plausible. It explains why you were all so nervous when I asked about the accident. I killed Rob. And from everything I know about myself, the wrong brother died in that crash.''

Amelia mumbled something about that being non-sense, but hadn't she felt the very same thing in her heart of hearts? Hadn't she been angry that his recklessness had cost a good man his life? She tried to touch Ryder, but for once he reeled away. With a last glance that nearly devoured her, he left the apartment. She heard his feet on the stairs as he ran from himself.

Hours passed. Amelia waited in the dark, her mind a windstorm of confusion. Impressions, both distant and recent, whirled about in her head.

Ryder cooking, swinging from a rope, looking down at her, the moon on his face, the sun in his hair. Ryder touching her, kissing her, struggling with his ethics, holding a preschooler, staring at the fetal monitor with tears rolling down his cheeks.

"Our baby," he had said.

"Our babies," she whispered aloud, as her daughters thumped around in the sanctuary she so willingly provided.

And then she was on her feet, searching the apartment for a flashlight, grabbing keys. She had to find Ryder.

The car was in the parking lot, so he was on foot or in a taxi. There was a heavy mist falling, so heavy, in fact, that she had to use the windshield wipers. She drove to Pepper's Place, a gut feeling telling her Ryder would seek a noisy, dark spot in which to hide. She walked through the smoky bar. She asked the bartender if he'd seen Ryder Hogan. A gruff, "Not for weeks," was his only answer.

She drove by his old schools, by the house in which he'd grown up. She didn't bother his parents or his brother because she knew he wouldn't retreat to them, not now, not with this. She drove by his office, hoping to see a light in the window, but the whole building was dark.

What next? The country club? The Mona Lisa?

No, those were places the old Ryder might run to lick his wounds.

Where would the new Ryder go?

And then Amelia knew....

Above the white line of the gentle surf, she saw the silhouette of a solitary figure sitting on the beach. Instinctively, Amelia knew it was Ryder.

The mist had turned to drizzle and she grabbed the flashlight and an umbrella from the back seat of the car. There was no other way, she decided as she struggled with the soft sand, to describe her trek across the beach other than as a waddle. She was glad there was no one to watch.

Ryder turned around when she was within ten feet of him. He reached up and steadied her as she folded her legs and sat down beside him. His hand was cold and wet and he released her immediately. Amelia set the flashlight on the sand between them and held the umbrella overhead.

After several moments of silence, she finally said, "I want you to know that you're wrong."

He turned to face her, the weirdly angled light reflecting off the planes of his damp cheeks. He said, "I read the newspaper, Amelia. I know I was the driver. And Hill said I was drunk. What irony! When I ran into Hill, I was down at police headquarters, determined to right my wrongs, completely unaware that my biggest wrong killed my own brother, that I'm a...a murderer."

"That's not what I'm talking about," Amelia said. All the feelings she had for him, both loving and angry, seemed to boil in her stomach. And then, as she touched his face, the anger mellowed to a dull ache.

"In everything you do, in every word you speak, you show the man you truly are," she whispered. "That old Ryder is gone. You chased him away. You were mistaken when you said the wrong brother died. You have two children on the way. How can you say the wrong man died?"

Her hand burned his cheek. The earth stopped spinning. Though her eyes were no more than glittering hollows on her heavily shadowed face, he sensed a fleeting recognition deep in his soul, something that throbbed between them, a connection as old as time.

He brought her hand from his cheek to his mouth, kissing each of her fingers, lingering, wanting the reality of his lips on her skin to stretch on forever. It was like being asleep, this amnesia thing, lost and stranded and so alone.

"Oh, Amelia," he murmured, "wake me with a kiss."

She leaned forward and kissed him, her lips warm and soft. She stared into his eyes, and he knew she was looking for confirmation that her kiss had done the trick, that it had yanked him from the fog.

But it hadn't. And suddenly, it didn't matter.

He was tired of the past. He was tired of the sordid details of a man he didn't know.

His past was lost. However, he needn't be lost.

All he had to do was make up his mind to go on from this time forward as a man of integrity. He could have a second chance, a new beginning. All he had to do was ask for it. If need be, beg for it! Starting now...

He fumbled in his pocket, then carefully withdrew the blue silk from the folds of tissue. Meeting Amelia's gaze, he said, "When I saw this, I thought of you, but that's not too unusual because I think about you all the time.

This is clumsy, Amelia…what I'm trying to say is, I love you. Marry me.''

He heard her sharp intake of breath.

''I mean it with all my heart,'' he said. ''I love you. I think you love me. I know you try not to, but bless your heart, you do love me, don't you?''

''Oh, Ryder,'' she finally mumbled.

''I love you so much,'' he said.

''You *think* you love me—''

''No, it's not pretend, it's not maybe. It's the real thing, Amelia. Like you said, I have children coming— we have children coming. I want to make something of my life, to create something that matters. Don't condemn me to a past that belongs to someone else. I need you.''

She stared at the scarf in his hands.

He said, ''Remember the other day when I asked you if I used to like the ocean? You said the point was, did I like it now? That was brilliant, Amelia. That was a turning point for me. And that's how I'm going to live.''

''Ryder—''

''Do you love me?'' he demanded. ''Forget about the man you once knew. Do you love the man sitting here with you on this wet beach, right now, tonight? Do you love *me*?''

The light glistened off her cheeks and he realized she was crying. Rain pitter-pattered on the umbrella she held above their heads, the retreating surf swished on the sand, but he barely heard any of it. He was waiting for another sound, a word that would make his life worth living.

She touched the scarf, met his eyes. Finally, almost as a sigh, she said it.

''Yes.''

Amelia wore the blue silk scarf to their first prenatal class. It didn't surprise her that she had the most attractive partner in the room, and she supposed by now, it shouldn't even surprise her that he was the most attentive.

What a journey he had traveled, she marveled as he helped her assume the correct posture and timed her make-believe contractions. He had made the transition from a self-serving rake to a caring mate, and he'd done it by using the deep reservoir of guts and courage he had possessed all along. She congratulated herself on being discerning enough to sense his potential right from the start.

And now she had consented to marry him, to make official a love that had created the life inside her body. It all felt so right, it was spooky. Once before, things had felt good like this—that had been the day he'd asked her to marry him...the first time.

But that hadn't been real.

Never mind. That was then, this was now. He loved her. He needed her. His feelings were genuine. She would stake her life on it.

She had loved him once before, but she realized that love had been naive, more a dream of what she wished than what he was. This time, she was in love with a real man, the man who had pledged himself to her and to their children. He'd grown, but in all fairness, so had she. And they'd made the trip together.

The wedding was planned for three weeks from that day as that was the soonest Aunt Jenny and Uncle Lou could leave the furniture store in Nevada and drive to Oregon for the ceremony. It was Ryder's idea to spring the news on his parents and brother while they gathered to celebrate his twenty-ninth birthday. As that was only a day away, she supposed she could wait, even though she was anxious to see Nina's face when she heard the news.

Everything was turning out perfectly!

So why did she still find herself worrying?

Perhaps it was because something still chased Ryder, still haunted him. They had decided to postpone sleeping in the same bed until after the babies came, but they didn't close their doors anymore and she could hear him tossing and turning and mumbling to himself.

Common sense said a day of reckoning would come. No matter. They would deal with it together.

Ryder was early getting dressed for his birthday party and Amelia had banished him to his room so she could finish decorating the apartment by herself.

Left to amuse himself, he decided to take a peek into one of the boxes filled with Rob's belongings.

The first was filled with books. Ryder picked up the top one, a children's classic, first edition. He carefully thumbed through the yellowing pages, smiling as he pictured himself reading it to his daughters. He was willing to bet his brother hadn't stored this book in a cardboard box, so he carefully placed it on a shelf.

With this book, he would pass along a piece of his brother to his daughters.

The next carton was layered with shirts still wrapped in their original plastic and items that appeared to have been taken off the top of a dresser. Among the old coins and tie clips, he spied a carved wooden box that looked like the one on top of his own bureau.

Sure enough, it seemed he and Rob had duplicate boxes in which to store their jewelry. He set the boxes side by side and wished he knew where they'd come from. Perhaps his mother would know, or his dad. He opened the lid on Rob's.

A knock on the door was followed by Amelia's voice. "Ryder? Philip and Sara just got here and your parents are on their way upstairs."

"Coming," he called, leaving the wood boxes for tonight.

"My father made them," Jack said moments later as he sneaked a taste of the frosting with his finger. "He made Philip a box, too, but because he was older than you twins, his is bigger."

"Which is only fair," Philip said with a grin.

Ryder was opening champagne, and just then, the cork flew off the bottle. The popping noise seemed somehow evocative and he stared at the cork where it had rolled under the table. Something clicked...corks...and weddings...then nothing. Another elusive clue evaporating into thin air.

Amelia passed around the glasses before proposing a toast for his birthday. It was his turn next, and joyfully, with his hands on Amelia's shoulders, he told his family about their plans to marry.

Patting her tummy, Amelia said, "I guess this is one bride who won't be wearing white."

"You can wear anything you want," Ryder said with a kiss on the back of her neck. "As long as you marry me."

Nina cried, "I knew it! I just knew it!"

Jack chortled, Philip delivered dire warnings about the pitfalls of marriage and was jabbed in the ribs by his new wife. The only note of discord was the way Ryder found his gaze returning over and over again to the blasted cork.

His father nervously presented him with a leather diary, monogrammed with his initials. "We know it's kind of different from what we usually get you," his dad said, "but, Ryder, you've changed, son, and we're proud of you."

"Thank you," he told his father, profoundly touched.

Philip and Sara gave him a new watch and Amelia presented him with a single red rose.

"It's the flower you gave me on our first date," she said, her eyes shining. "But this one also comes with a certificate at Rose's art gallery for a family portrait." She patted her tummy and added, "To be done in a few months, of course."

Overwhelmed, he kissed her dewy lips. As they all sang to him, he held the flower to his nose. The heavy perfume went right to his head, and for a second, he had the overwhelming urge to stuff the bud in his pocket. His hands trembled and his head felt light.

Amelia looked up at him. "What's wrong?"

"I don't know," he said.

"You look odd."

"It's nothing," he told her, though he couldn't help but think that something was happening to him that might change everything.

Hours later, he stood in her doorway, watching her sleep. His own slumber was so uneasy that her peaceful repose fascinated him. Slowly, he entered her room and silently approached her bed. Then he lay down beside her and she turned toward him.

He gathered her in his arms and she smiled, but her eyes stayed closed and he doubted she even awoke. Maybe he was part of a dream for her. He kissed her brow and hoped so.

For some time, he lay there, the moonlight creating a soft glow in the room, Amelia's breathing steady and calm, one of his daughters wiggling beneath his right hand. Amelia's hair smelled like roses and he closed his eyes....

It was dark and he was in a car...racing...free. A mirror beside him, mocking...

He came awake with a start, mouth dry, heart pounding. This time he'd managed to stay in the dream long enough to look in the mirror.

There had been no reflection, just a swirling void.

Troubled, Ryder carefully extricated himself from Amelia's arms, but not carefully enough.

"Ryder?" she mumbled, her eyes half open.

"It's okay, go back to sleep," he told her, smoothing her golden hair away from her forehead.

"You okay?"

"I'm fine," he said, kissing her brow, loving her so much it hurt. "Go to sleep."

He waited until she relaxed again, then went back to his own room, his heart still knocking against his ribs.

The rosebud lay on his nightstand and he stared at it, still not sure why it bothered him. He wanted to throw it away, but he couldn't bring himself to do it. Instead, as a distraction, he investigated the contents of Rob's box. A watch with the engraved initials RJH, Robert Joseph Hogan. Heavy gold cuff links, a medallion. And then a ring caught his eye, a gold band with a polished onyx stone that jiggled slightly in its setting.

No engraving, a modest affair, really. He glanced at the rose again. Then he looked at his own hand and the signet ring given back to him after the accident.

As though he was caught in another dream, he replaced his ring with Rob's.

How long did he sit there staring at his hand? How long before he picked up the rosebud and squeezed it in his fist? How long before the distant voice of an argument raced through his mind, a wedding, music, Amelia in blue, Rob, a red rose tossed aside on a platter of champagne flutes?

The images came faster and faster, spinning in Ryder's head, a kaleidoscope he couldn't stop.

He was standing at the window now, staring out at the breaking dawn, the bud still in his fist, the signet ring abandoned on the comforter.

So far, he'd remembered a reading chair, a rope swing, a window seat, the beach, cuff links in a wooden box, Amelia in blue.

The only thing all his memories had in common was that they were memories shared with Rob. Boyhood places, identical boxes…Amelia.

His head reeled as daylight and memories broke at the same time.

Amelia at the club…pregnant…the anger, the fear, the argument…

Damn that man! When would he start taking responsibility for his actions? When would he stop hurting people?

And this woman, delicate, vulnerable. He'd known she was special from the first moment he saw her, the very first moment. He recalled the feeling of destiny as she approached, the bounding joy that had swelled in his heart when she spoke…and then the disappointment.

She was already taken, already pregnant.

With Ryder's child!

He walked to the mirror. In his dream he'd had no reflection.…

He stared into his own brown eyes. He saw the same shaggy dark hair, the same nose, lips and chin that had greeted him every day since he could recall.

He saw Rob.

All along, he'd been waiting for a pivotal moment, a shining light, something traumatic or sensational to happen that would herald back his past. A bump on the head, another accident...

He hadn't expected it to sneak up on him, blindsiding him with its subtlety.

It didn't matter. His memory was coming back as surely as the tide swept up the beach every twelve hours.

He gazed at his image and he knew.

Ryder Hogan died in the crash.

The man staring at his reflection was Rob Hogan.

He was Rob Hogan.

Chapter Ten

Memories collided with each other in their headlong rush to be known. While at first images were jumbled and out of sequence, eventually Rob pieced together the night of the accident.

Rob. He was Rob.

It still caused him a moment's pause to think of himself as Rob instead of Ryder....

Ryder was drunk, but drunk or sober, he was also stubborn. Rob could clearly remember his determination not to let Ryder drive off alone. He could remember throwing himself in the car.

Convinced Amelia was trying to trap him, Ryder had sworn she wouldn't get away with it. Rob had sat there, white-knuckled, rage growing inside him until it was like a cement truck parked on his chest.

"You're never going to change!" he'd exploded. "You take what you want, you always have. Look at you, big man in the community. You're still wearing *my* fraternity ring. I know you filched it when they kicked you out. It didn't really matter to me. It didn't hurt anyone to let you have your little fantasy. But now you've stolen a woman's heart and body for the same selfish reasons, and it's ruthless.''

Lost in his fury, he was hardly aware that Ryder had turned off onto a remote logging road. After a few miles, after a new round of arguments, Ryder abruptly stopped the car, tore off the signet ring and threw it at Rob. Rob could clearly recall the ping of metal as it hit the inside of the passenger door before being swallowed by the shadows on the floor.

Then Ryder staggered from the car, determined to duke it out. With one slow-motion punch delivered to no one, he crumbled to the ground before Rob could even reach him.

Disgusted, Rob dragged Ryder around to the passenger side. That was when he saw the ring on the carpet. As he'd stopped wearing his own onyx ring just the week before due to a loose stone, he slipped this one on his finger.

And that, he now realized, was where the mistaken identity started—the ring Ryder had worn for years now on Rob's finger, switched positions in the car, facial cuts they both suffered, Rob sentimentally stuffing Ryder's red boutonniere in his pocket because it had touched Amelia's face, identical clothes and haircuts, bungled lab tests. Even his mother's preoccupation with his father's health had made her less astute than usual.

Rob sat on the edge of the bed. His head vibrated with tension as he recalled navigating the maze of dirt roads, hopelessly lost, then Ryder waking from his stupor and grabbing the steering wheel. They fought, but Ryder had leverage on his side and the car soon jetted off the road, down an embankment. Trees whizzed by, a river—and then a merciful blank until consciousness returned and he found himself in the hospital, Amelia waiting for him....

Not for him.

For Ryder.

For the father of her children.

Not him. Ryder.

He felt his eyes burn. Were these tears of relief because he wasn't, after all, guilty of killing his brother? Tears of regret because good or bad, drunk or sober, Ryder had been his twin? Or were they tears of sorrow for Amelia and what all of this was going to mean to her?

To them.

She was in love with Ryder. Not him.

And his parents had buried him, mourned him.

Everything he worked for was gone. His law practice—unless Julia was managing to keep it going without him—his house, his car, all his books, gone.

Even Socrates, the snippy little dog he'd been baby-sitting while his professor friend was on a teaching sabbatical in England, had been absorbed into another home.

He had to get his old life back...but how?

Amelia stood on Ryder's balcony, her hands resting on top of the "shelf" her pregnancy provided. She stared out at the bay and wished she understood what was going on.

Two weeks before, Ryder had come into her room during the night. He'd slipped into her bed, folded her in his arms, and held her tightly.

Or had it been a dream?

By morning, her bed had been empty. She had found him sitting at the table, a duffel bag by his feet, a look on his face that alarmed her.

He told her his memory was coming back. She'd been

expecting this news, knowing that the event would bring as much pain as joy, but equally convinced it wouldn't change anything between them. In the next breath, he added he was leaving town for a few days.

Standing then, he'd pulled her into his arms and kissed her like he never had before, with acute longing, with aching sorrow, with hopeless passion.

Or had that, too, been a dream?

When she'd said, "Ryder," he'd looked at her as though she'd kicked him.

Four days later, he was back with no explanation as to where he'd been. But he wasn't the same. He wasn't the old Ryder and he wasn't the new Ryder. Though he was pleasant with her, he was also detached, as though preparing for the day she left him or he left her. He'd stopped going into his office, spending long hours instead locked away in his room, going through Rob's boxes, Rob's onyx ring on his finger.

She went back inside. For once, his door was ajar and she gently pushed it open, knocking as she did so.

He was sitting crossed-legged on the floor, a box of Rob's books before him, one volume open in his hands.

"We need to talk," she said.

"Not now—"

"Yes, now. If we're getting married in a few days, you're going to have to start explaining yourself. Like this sudden morbid fascination with Rob's things. Is it guilt that you're responsible for his death? Would it help to go back and talk with Dr. Bass?"

He stared at her. She felt suddenly uneasy, as though she was looking at a stranger. He was scaring her.

"You're right, we have to talk," he said. "I've been wrong to let things slide this long."

Now she didn't want to talk. She left his room.

He followed. He gripped her wrist and she turned to face him. He said, "I wasn't going to tell you about this until after the babies were born, but you're right, we can't get married until you know."

"Know what?" she whispered.

Again he stared. Then finally, he sighed deeply. "I think you'd better sit down."

"Ryder!"

At the mention of his name, he winced. "Sit down," he pleaded.

"What do you have to tell me that's so bad I have to sit down? That you don't love me anymore, is that it?" Wiping tears from her eyes, she added, "I knew this would happen. Damn it, I let you sweet talk me—"

He grabbed her arms. "Amelia, stop! Let me explain. You have to know—"

"Know what?" she demanded, voice trembling.

After an interminable pause, his words shattered everything. "Amelia, honey, Ryder is...dead. I'm Rob."

"No," she protested.

"Amelia—"

"This is just some elaborate scheme to get out of marrying me. Well, don't think—"

He made her sit beside him. As gently as he could, he told her about the accident and about his recent trip to California and how he'd gone to see his physician who had checked his records.

"I broke my toe a few months ago. I don't think Mom and Dad even knew about it, but the doctor took an x-ray and sure enough...there's no doubt, Amelia. This isn't some game I'm playing. I went right to my office, as well. My name's been sanded off the front door, but Julia knew me immediately and, more importantly, I knew her." He tried not to think of the stunned expression on his partner's face when he walked in unannounced. He'd been afraid the shock would send her into premature labor.

Amelia still looked unconvinced.

"The first time I saw you was at Philip's wedding. I remember the sound of champagne corks flying. You were wearing a blue dress. You were breathtaking, I couldn't take my eyes off of you. You came up to me. I thought you were flirting and I was thrilled, but then you confessed you were carrying Ryder's baby. That's the first time I had to tell you I wasn't Ryder. This is the second time. But, darling, none of this changes the way I feel about you."

"Ryder is dead," she said woodenly, as though it was just now sinking in.

"He's been dead for months."

"No," she said. "To me, he's been dead for ten minutes."

"Amelia, listen to me. What we feel for each other started after the accident. Nothing has changed."

Her laugh startled him. "Of course, things have changed," she cried.

"I am exactly who I was two weeks ago—"

"No. Two weeks ago, you were Ryder. I was carrying *your* babies. Then your memory returned, and you became secretive and withdrawn. You're a stranger to me."

He yearned to hold on to her hands, to pin her in place. It had been wrong to go off by himself, to try to sort through what he'd learned without consulting her. He wanted her to trust him, and yet he hadn't trusted her.

"I was floored when I realized what happened," he said. "I needed time to adjust, to figure out how to reclaim my life. In one fell swoop, I learned who I really was, I mourned my brother, and I realized my parents had sold off my life. And you, of course. I was afraid what you would do.''

She stood abruptly, no small feat given her current condition. ''Stop! I don't want to hear this. You said you needed time. So do I.''

''But the wedding—''

''There isn't going to be a wedding, Ryder. Rob.'' Tears welled in her eyes as she added, ''I don't even know what to call you!''

He was standing by now and he put his arms around her. ''It'll get easier with time, sweetheart. You'll see. What you have to remember is this.'' And with that he kissed her, putting all his longing, all his fear, all his hope, all of himself into the pressure of his lips on hers, willing her to see that what they had together hadn't changed.

She almost stumbled in her effort to get away from him. ''I need time,'' she repeated. ''You need time. My God, you have to tell your parents...and the police.''

''I know—''

''I'm going to Nevada,'' she said.

''Nevada!''

''I have a house there. It was my plan all along. Aunt Jenny and Uncle Lou will help me.''

He didn't dare touch her. ''Amelia, listen to me. You can't travel, you're too far along. The doctor warned us that twins are often early. Besides, I promised to marry you and help raise these babies. It's a promise I intend to honor.''

The look she gave him convinced him he'd managed to say the wrong thing. She mumbled, ''You're under no obligation.''

''I know that—''

"And you have no claim on me...or my children. Absolutely none."

Her words wounded him. He blinked a couple of times, bitter tears stinging his eyes.

Then she was gone.

She locked her door and started tearing clothes out of drawers and off shelves, the world a blur through her tears. Halfway through her packing, she sat on the bed and buried her head in her hands, harrowing sobs racking her body. The babies seemed ominously still. Ryder's babies. But Ryder was dead.

It was like losing him twice. She mourned the old and the new Ryder. She mourned lost love.

Not lost, an inner voice whispered. He's still here. He's just got a different name. And a different past...

But Rob was here because he thought he should be.

She recalled the day they'd met, the terror of realizing that her feelings for Ryder had escalated, not diminished. But what she'd felt hadn't been for Ryder—it had been for Rob.

She hadn't loved Ryder for months and months, not since his actions following their supposed engagement had shown him for the man he truly was. Everything she felt for the man standing outside her door had started at Philip's wedding and continued to build after the accident—just as he'd said.

But it didn't matter. Rob could say whatever he wanted, but his true feelings had come out when he told her he intended to honor his promise.

The doorknob rattled. "Amelia, be reasonable. You can't drive alone!"

"Go away," she said, resuming her packing.

"No."

She threw into her bag the white sleeper with the embroidered ducks, the pink blanket she'd been working on for weeks, and a few things for herself. She paused when her fingers touched the blue scarf that Ryder—Rob—had given her. She'd always thought of it as an engagement gift. She took it, too.

Standing there, waiting for the courage to open the door, she felt warm water trickling down her legs.

"Oh no," she moaned. "No, no, no. Not now, no."

But the sensation continued, followed by the first small contraction. It looked as though her daughters were determined to be born in Oregon. More tears ran down her cheeks as she tried her breathing techniques and failed. She opened the door.

"It's time," she said.

It took Rob a few seconds to grasp her meaning. "The babies?"

"You'd better drive me to the hospital."

"I'll call the doctor first," he said, his voice tinged with alarm.

"Just hurry."

As he ran to the phone and made the call, Amelia grabbed a towel from the bathroom and picked up her suitcase. Rob quickly returned and took it from her, their hands brushing. He leaned over and kissed her cheek.

"This doesn't change anything except the timing," she warned him. "I'm not staying. As soon as I...as we...can travel—"

"Let's talk about all of this later," he said.

For a second, their gazes held. She was thinking that he wasn't actually the father of her children, that he had a whole life in California, maybe even a girlfriend. Maybe that was why he had left so suddenly, to tell the true love of his life that he couldn't see her anymore because there was this blonde up in Oregon who his brother had knocked up. So sorry, but family obligations and all that, you understand.

"Who is Julia?"

His eyebrows inched up his forehead, but he must have correctly deciphered the have-to-know look in her eyes because he said, "My law partner."

"Is that all she is?"

"Well, she's an old girlfriend—"

His words were lost as another contraction gripped her.

"Take a deep breath," he coached. "Remember to focus. Here—squeeze my hand, that's good."

She did as he directed, his calm voice the thread that pulled her to the other side of the contraction.

"Honey, it's time to go," he said gently.

How right he was.

"You're doing great," Rob said.

She glowered at him. Part of her wanted to tell him to go away. The reality of the situation was that she had never been intimate with this man and here he was coaching her through childbirth.

Some first date.

"Now push again," the doctor said. Amelia dug her fingernails into Rob's arm and pushed.

A cry so compelling that Amelia's heart broke in two announced the birth of her first daughter.

"She's perfect!" the doctor said as she cradled the baby in her arms, showing her to Amelia and Rob. Amelia saw the same longing to hold the baby in Rob's eyes that she felt in her own heart. Too miserable to think ahead to the future, she murmured, "I'm going to name her Chloe, after my mother."

Rob clutched her shoulder. She didn't dare look at his

face again. All she could think about was his comment
that Julia had been his girlfriend. Hadn't Nina said Julia
was six or seven months pregnant? Was Julia carrying
Rob's baby? Was that why he knew so much about pregnancy?

"Let me touch her," Amelia said.

The nurse brought the baby close to Amelia's face.
Chloe was pink and perfect, like an opening bud. Amelia
had always thought she would look at her baby and see
her own features or maybe Ryder's, but this child was an
individual unto herself.

Her skin felt like nothing Amelia had ever touched
before. Silk, maybe. Fine and smooth and lovely.

Amelia felt a love so strong, it shook the very foun-
dations of her soul.

With Amelia's eyes tracking her every movement, the
nurse whisked Chloe to the far side of the room to weigh
and measure her. Rob patted Amelia's damp forehead
with a cloth, then gave her a sip of water.

The doctor said, "One more to go, kiddo."

More coaching, more pushing, a soft, throaty cry, and
then Amelia delivered another baby. Her euphoria was
tempered by the stillness in the room. She imagined every
conceivable horror until the doctor chuckled.

"I goofed, Amelia. Not two girls—a girl and a boy.
And this little guy looks just like his daddy!"

Everyone turned to look at Rob, including Amelia.
Tears streamed down his face as he stared at his nephew.
Amelia's heart ached. These should be his children, she
thought. *His* children.

She turned back to her dark-haired son who was amazingly composed. He, too, was petal soft, darker than his
sister, beautiful. For a second, it seemed his gaze met and
held Amelia's, and she felt tears burn her nose and pud-

dle in her eyes as she sensed the beginning of their life-
long relationship.

"What's his name?" the doctor asked.

"Ryder," Rob said. "After his father."

Momentarily stunned, Amelia looked up at Rob who
was still staring at his nephew.

"You'll have a junior in the family," the doctor said.
Rob didn't answer.

They brought Amelia's babies to her, two small bodies
swaddled in white cotton, one wearing a blue knit cap,
the other pink. As if she couldn't tell them apart! Chloe
was fair and almost hairless, tiny and as delicate as a
flower. She cried until Amelia nursed her, but something
told Amelia that this baby was going to be a handful.

Ryder, on the other hand, was longer, darker and qui-
eter. He blinked a few times as a nurse held him close
so Amelia could grasp his tiny starfish hand and gaze
into his dark eyes. He reminded her of his father.

No—not his father, his uncle. He reminded her of Rob.

She turned to tell him this.

He was gone.

Rob sat by Amelia's bed and anticipated her awakening, just as she had awaited his so long ago. There were
two bassinets in the room, holding his niece and nephew,
both sound asleep like their mother. It would be hard to
find a more peaceful place on earth than this room, he
thought, with these people. Except that his stomach was
churning up battery acid because he was afraid that
within the hour, he would lose them all forever.

Oh, Amelia.

As if she'd heard him calling her name, Amelia's gray
eyes fluttered open and zeroed in on him.

"My babies—"

"They're right here, sleeping. They're beautiful."

She sat up and peered at her children, her lips spreading into a smile that would have illuminated a small city. It faded as she turned back to him. "Rob, you left so suddenly. Where did you go?"

"I went to tell my parents about the babies, but also about Ryder. You can imagine what a shock it was. It'll take some adjusting, but in the end, they'll be fine, I'll help them. Then I went to Ryder's office to clear things up there and to warn them that I intend to let the DA know about Dalton's true whereabouts on the night of the fire."

"You've been busy."

He laughed. "All of this pales compared to the talk I'm going to have with Detective Hill. He's never going to believe me."

Amelia looked down at her hands. "Rob, who's Julia?"

"I told you, she's my law partner."

"And your girlfriend?"

"That was over a long time ago."

"But she's pregnant."

"She has a husband, Amelia. For three years now. A nice guy. You'll like him."

She smiled again, this time for him. He wondered if he would ever get used to the way her smile ignited his heart. He rather doubted it.

One of the babies awoke with a soft but imperious cry that startled Amelia and galvanized Rob. He discovered it was Chloe who fussed and he gently lifted her into his arms. It was the first time in his life he had held a newborn child and he was stunned by the way his heart seemed to give his hands direction. He kissed her sweet forehead.

"Here's your daughter, Amelia."

"Chloe," Amelia said, her eyes warm and soft. "She reminds me of my mother, small and fair and determined." She kissed the baby's cheek, and Rob felt his breath catch. Looking up at him, she murmured, "Her brother looks just like you."

"Well, Ryder and I were identical twins, you know. Our genetic makeup is damn near the same. I hope you don't mind that I took the liberty of naming him."

"No," she said. Chloe had fallen asleep again, against Amelia's breasts. She was studying the baby's hands and feet, her fingers gentle against the newborn skin. What a picture they made! He tried to freeze-frame it in his brain.

From the bassinet, Ryder whimpered. Rob immediately rescued him. The baby stopped fretting as he fixed his somber dark eyes on Rob's face.

He was a beautiful boy.

He's going to need a father, Rob thought.

"They're both going to need a father."

He was barely aware he had said this out loud until Amelia responded.

"You're trying to assume Ryder's responsibility," she said, her voice shaky. "It isn't necessary. We'll be okay."

He gingerly sat down on the chair pulled up close to Amelia's bed. The baby held tightly against one shoulder, he placed a hand on her cheek. "Listen to me carefully," he began. "When my memory first came back, I was thrilled to be me again. I wanted my old life back, my own identity. That's why I went to California. Even though Mom and Dad did a pretty thorough job of organizing my affairs after my supposed death, it can all be reversed. I could leave today and pick up the pieces and within a month recapture the life I built for myself."

"When are you going?" she asked softly.

"See, that's the rub. Because during my amnesia, I changed. I fell in love. My life down there now seems outdated, a poor fit for a man with a family. Amelia, do you understand what I'm saying to you?"

He could see indecision warring in her eyes. She still didn't believe his motives.

"I'm saying I love you," he explained in case childbirth had left her dazed. "And if the only way you'll take me is as an amnesiac, then I'll bang my head against a rock or fall into a ravine, whatever it takes."

"You love me," she said with wonder in her voice.

"That's right. I've loved you with unwavering certainty since the day we met. I asked you once before, Amelia. I'm asking you again. Do you love me? Do you love the man before you now?"

Amelia gazed into brown eyes that had always had a way of delving into her heart. This man was so much like Ryder with his confidence and playfulness, and yet so very different.

Did he mean what he was saying? How ironic that the very qualities that made him honorable also made her doubt him.

He smiled the pure, wonderful smile that she had first loved in Ryder, the smile that seemed to spring from his soul. But this smile was on Rob's face, and because it was, and because she knew who he was in a sense that totally eclipsed what she had ever really known of Ryder, it filled her with longing.

Was he being honest with himself and with her?

Had he ever once been dishonest?

Never.

Then wasn't the logical conclusion that he was speaking the truth, that he truly did love her?

She furrowed her brow and studied his eyes, constantly reminding herself that she and this man had no past beyond that which started right in this very same hospital. What he had shown himself to be was what he was, what she loved. Period.

She recalled wondering once why he had hidden from her the part of himself that she now found so enchanting. Now she knew he hadn't hidden a thing.

The smile slid from his face, replaced with an intense look of anxiety. This was his look alone. She suspected only a man who had already lost everything once in his life could realize what was at stake now.

"You asked me once if I would wake you with a kiss," she told him, her fingers closing over his. "My darling, that's what you've done for me. How in the world could I not love you?"

"Then you'll marry me?"

"Yes," she told him. "Of course."

Juggling babies, they managed to find each other's lips. The kiss was full of wonder and discovery, and for some time afterward, they stared at each other as though it was hard to break the connection they had just renewed in their heart of hearts. He kissed her again.

Amelia pulled away when she heard a commotion in the hallway. "What's that?"

Rob looked slightly embarrassed. "In a couple of seconds, that door is going to pop open. Mom and Dad are bringing the preacher, Philip is bringing champagne, I brought the marriage license and this."

He carefully reached in a pocket located under his nephew's slumbering body and withdrew a twinkling ring which he slid on Amelia's finger. Amelia found graceful golden petals encasing a diamond.

"Do you mind too much that your aunt and uncle can't

be here? We could delay things if you want. It's your call.''

She straightened up slightly, adjusting gown and baby. ''The four of us are here—I suppose that's all that really counts. Oh, Rob, is this really happening?''

''You bet it is.''

She tilted his face until he was looking into her eyes. She needed to say one more thing. ''I adore you, Rob. And from this moment on, as far as I'm concerned, Chloe and Ryder are your babies as much as they're mine. They're our babies, together, four arms to hold them, just like you said.''

She wiped a tear from his cheek as he lowered his head and kissed her again. She wanted the kiss to last forever and ever....

The door burst open then and both babies awoke simultaneously.

After that, it was a wedding like most others, complete with a best man and a bridesmaid, one wearing a blue cap, one wearing pink, both a little on the fussy side and passed from one adoring adult to the next. There were flowers rescued from the nurses' station, a handsome groom in a borrowed shirt, and a bride, who, thanks to the bleached cotton sheet pulled up under her chin, wore white.

But more importantly, there were promises made and vows exchanged, lingering looks, tears, tender kisses— all in all, a perfect combination of custom and improvisation...with a touch of kismet thrown in for good measure.

*   *   *   *   *

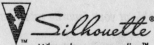

SILHOUETTE'S 20TH ANNIVERSARY CONTEST
OFFICIAL RULES
NO PURCHASE NECESSARY TO ENTER

1. To enter, follow directions published in the offer to which you are responding. Contest begins 1/1/00 and ends on 8/24/00 (the "Promotion Period"). Method of entry may vary. Mailed entries must be postmarked by 8/24/00, and received by 8/31/00.

2. During the Promotion Period, the Contest may be presented via the Internet. Entry via the Internet may be restricted to residents of certain geographic areas that are disclosed on the Web site. To enter via the Internet, if you are a resident of a geographic area in which Internet entry is permissible, follow the directions displayed on-line, including typing your essay of 100 words or fewer telling us "Where In The World Your Love Will Come Alive." On-line entries must be received by 11:59 p.m. Eastern Standard time on 8/24/00. Limit one e-mail entry per person, household and e-mail address per day, per presentation. If you are a resident of a geographic area in which entry via the Internet is permissible, you may, in lieu of submitting an entry on-line, enter by mail, by hand-printing your name, address, telephone number and contest number/name on an 8"x 11" plain piece of paper and telling us in 100 words or fewer "Where In The World Your Love Will Come Alive," and mailing via first-class mail to: Silhouette 20th Anniversary Contest, (in the U.S.) P.O. Box 9069, Buffalo, NY 14269-9069; (In Canada) P.O. Box 637, Fort Erie, Ontario, Canada L2A 5X3. Limit one 8"x 11" mailed entry per person, household and e-mail address per day. <u>On-line and/or 8"x 11" mailed entries received from persons residing in geographic areas in which Internet entry is not permissible will be disqualified.</u> No liability is assumed for lost, late, incomplete, inaccurate, nondelivered or misdirected mail, or misdirected e-mail, for technical, hardware or software failures of any kind, lost or unavailable network connection, or failed, incomplete, garbled or delayed computer transmission or any human error which may occur in the receipt or processing of the entries in the contest.

3. Essays will be judged by a panel of members of the Silhouette editorial and marketing staff based on the following criteria:

   Sincerity (believability, credibility)—50%

   Originality (freshness, creativity)—30%

   Aptness (appropriateness to contest ideas)—20%

   Purchase or acceptance of a product offer does not improve your chances of winning. In the event of a tie, duplicate prizes will be awarded.

4. All entries become the property of Harlequin Enterprises Ltd., and will not be returned. Winner will be determined no later than 10/31/00 and will be notified by mail. Grand Prize winner will be required to sign and return Affidavit of Eligibility within 15 days of receipt of notification. Noncompliance within the time period may result in disqualification and an alternative winner may be selected. All municipal, provincial, federal, state and local laws and regulations apply. Contest open only to residents of the U.S. and Canada who are 18 years of age or older, and is void wherever prohibited by law. Internet entry is restricted solely to residents of those geographical areas in which Internet entry is permissible. Employees of Torstar Corp., their affiliates, agents and members of their immediate families are not eligible. Taxes on the prizes are the sole responsibility of winners. Entry and acceptance of any prize offered constitutes permission to use winner's name, photograph or other likeness for the purposes of advertising, trade and promotion on behalf of Torstar Corp. without further compensation to the winner, unless prohibited by law. Torstar Corp and D.L. Blair, Inc., their parents, affiliates and subsidiaries, are not responsible for errors in printing or electronic presentation of contest or entries. In the event of printing or other errors which may result in unintended prize values or duplication of prizes, all affected contest materials or entries shall be null and void. If for any reason the Internet portion of the contest is not capable of running as planned, including infection by computer virus, bugs, tampering, unauthorized intervention, fraud, technical failures, or any other causes beyond the control of Torstar Corp. which corrupt or affect the administration, secrecy, fairness, integrity or proper conduct of the contest, Torstar Corp. reserves the right, at its sole discretion, to disqualify any individual who tampers with the entry process and to cancel, terminate, modify or suspend the contest or the Internet portion thereof. In the event of a dispute regarding an on-line entry, the entry will be deemed submitted by the authorized holder of the e-mail account submitted at the time of entry. Authorized account holder is defined as the natural person who is assigned to an e-mail address by an Internet access provider, on-line service provider or other organization that is responsible for arranging e-mail address for the domain associated with the submitted e-mail address.

5. Prizes: Grand Prize—a $10,000 vacation to anywhere in the world. Travelers (at least one must be 18 years of age or older) or parent or guardian if one traveler is a minor, must sign and return a Release of Liability prior to departure. Travel must be completed by December 31, 2001, and is subject to space and accommodations availability. Two hundred (200) Second Prizes—a two-book limited edition autographed collector set from one of the Silhouette Anniversary authors: Nora Roberts, Diana Palmer, Linda Howard or Annette Broadrick (value $10.00 each set). All prizes are valued in U.S. dollars.

6. For a list of winners (available after 10/31/00), send a self-addressed, stamped envelope to: Harlequin Silhouette 20th Anniversary Winners, P.O. Box 4200, Blair, NE 68009-4200.

Contest sponsored by Torstar Corp., P.O. Box 9042, Buffalo, NY 14269-9042.